Linebacker Blitz

Linebacker Blitz

by Bill J. Carol

Steck-Vaughn Company • Austin, Texas
An Intext Publisher

ISBN 0-8114-7734-7
Library of Congress Catalog Card Number 79–151705

Chapter One

PETE DENNIS WATCHED the Potsdam quarterback approach the line of scrimmage. For an instant the quarterback looked directly across the line at Pete. Then he looked straight ahead and began to bark out his signals. Pete backed up a step, took the gamble, and started his blitz.

A split second before Pete broke across the line of scrimmage, the ball was snapped. The quarterback spun away from Pete and handed off to the fullback attempting a quick plunge up the middle. Pete moved swiftly into the fullback's path, put his shoulder down, and met the fullback's charge headon. The collision jarred Pete, and he felt his chin strap give way as his helmet snapped back. But he kept driving forward and slammed the back to the ground a full yard behind the line of scrimmage.

As Pete got to his feet, there was no way for him to keep himself from grinning. With his helmet slightly askew, a portion of his thick, reddish-brown hair was visible. His jaw was solid with just the trace of a cleft, his cheekbones high and prominent. At the moment the smile that lit his face caused his dark eyes to glow with a mischievous light.

"Nice play," said Gooberman. "But who told you to blitz on that down?"

Pete shrugged. "After all, Gooberman. I'm just filling in at linebacker. I didn't know I was supposed to get permission every time I blitzed."

Gooberman, the monsterman who was also the team's defensive captain, grinned. "Oh, no. Of course you didn't. But now you do."

Pete adjusted his helmet, snapped his chin strap, then turned to wait for the Potsdam huddle to break. Ordinarily Pete was the team's regular left tackle. But an injury that looked like a sprained ankle had side-lined Frenchy Wells, Canton's first-string middle linebacker. As a result, since the end of the third period, Pete had found himself trying to master the intricacies of a new defensive position. And now, after that last play, he was beginning to think he just might be able to handle the job—at least until this game ended.

It was third and six. The Potsdam Royals were down by three touchdowns, but with only ten minutes left in the game, they were anxious to get something on the scoreboard.

The Potsdam huddle broke. Pete watched the quarterback approach the line. As soon as the fellow began calling signals, Pete moved as if he might charge through the line again, then backed off. At that instant, the quarterback took the snap and backpedaled quickly, his passing arm held high and ready.

"Pass!" Gooberman called. "Pass!"

Swiftly Pete drifted back into the hook zone. He saw Potsdam's tight end cutting across the flat just in front of him. Pete tried to come back, but was too late. The pass was on target. The end tucked it away securely, turned, and cut up field.

Then Pete met him.

What happened after that was difficult to say. All that Pete could remember clearly was putting his head down and reaching out to grab the end. The next thing he knew, he was flying backward. The sky exchanged places with the field, something heavy struck Pete in the back, and for a moment he had difficulty sucking in his breath. Then, shaking his head, he sat up just in time to catch a glimpse of the end slicing into the right corner of the end zone.

As Pete shook his head again and got groggily to

his feet, he found it difficult to collect his thoughts.

"You all right, Pete?"

Pete turned. Gooberman, a concerned frown on his face, was looking intently at Pete.

Pete continued shaking his head in an effort to clear away the cobwebs. "I'm all right, I guess. But how come they let steamrollers on the field during a game?"

"That end *is* a lot of horse, I've got to admit," Gooberman said, grinning. "You sure you're all right?"

"He ran right over me."

"I know."

"Like I wasn't even there."

"You were there. You slowed him down a little."

"Sure I did."

Gooberman shrugged. "He's a good runner."

Gary West's effort to duplicate the Potsdam quarterback's performance got him only as far as the Canton 45. With six minutes left in the ball game, West punted. Potsdam ran it back to their forty, and as Pete jogged out onto the field, he could not help noticing the eagerness of the Potsdam offensive unit. For all intents and purposes, the game was over. They couldn't possibly get two touchdowns in the time remaining.

But as they hupped up to the line a moment later, eagerness and confidence fairly oozed out of each player. It was momentarily unnerving and caused Pete to become just a little uncertain as the Potsdam quarterback began to shout his signals.

The ball was snapped. The quarterback spun to hand off the ball to his halfback. Pete moved to fill the off-tackle hole. But as he did so, he was hit from the right side, hard. He felt himself sprawling sideways, then collapsing as he tripped over a tangle of tumbling bodies. He tried to reach back, but the Potsdam halfback was already past him through the hole and galloping for daylight.

The scatback got as far as the Canton forty, for a twenty-yard gain. As Pete pulled himself to his feet, he could only shake his head in frustration. They'd really taken him out of that play. Well, he'd be waiting for them the next time they tried that one.

The try came in the next play. Again the quarterback spun about and handed off to his halfback. But this time Pete moved into the off-tackle hole with lightning speed and met the little back head on. The two crunched together like a couple of bucks in springtime. The Potsdam back gave ground, and Pete threw him to the turf a full yard behind the line of scrimmage.

But as he pulled himself off his victim, he noticed that all the action was elsewhere. The back was grinning up at him.

"That quarterback of ours sure can fake, can't he," the fellow said.

Pete whirled in time to see the other Potsdam halfback being knocked out of bounds on the twenty.

On the next play the quarterback pitched out to his fullback. As the big fellow tucked the ball under his arm and started lugging for the right corner, Pete hurdled over a lunging blocker and pursued the back laterally along the other side of the line of scrimmage.

The right linebacker, Johnny Robbins, was cut down just in front of Pete by the Potsdam guard leading the play. That left it up to Pete. He hand-wrestled his way past one would-be blocker and found himself with a clear shot at the ballcarrier. The fellow grinned at Pete behind his nose guard and put his head down.

For just an instant Pete hesitated, then lowered his shoulder and tried to cut the back down with a block. Pete felt his shoulder glance off the back's plunging thigh. Then he slammed into the ground. When he stopped rolling and looked downfield, he saw the back attempt to straight-arm Gooberman. Gooberman caught the boy's arm and spun him to the ground. But now it was first and ten on Canton's ten-yard line.

"I should have had him," said Pete, shaking his head unhappily as the defensive huddle closed about him.

Gooberman looked at him, as did the others in the huddle. "That's right. You should have. You had a fine shot at him."

"I dived for him, but all I came up with was air."

"He's a pretty fancy runnner, all right," Gooberman said. Then he looked around the huddle. "Stay loose. Be ready for anything."

The Potsdam huddle broke. The quarterback followed his center to the line of scrimmage and glanced for just a moment at his tight end.

"Pass!" Pete hissed softly to Gooberman out of the corner of his mouth.

Then, as the quarterback started his count, Pete made like he was charging through the line. At the last moment he pulled up and appeared to relax. Then he started through again—and this time he kept going just as the ball was snapped.

The quarterback raced back and turned. But Pete had slipped past his blockers and had stayed with him all the time. Head down, he rammed into the quarterback before the fellow could get the ball up over his shoulder. Pete heard the fellow grunt, felt him going down under him, and continued to drive, both arms wrapped tightly about the back's waist.

They hit the ground with a numbing thud. Pete heard the quarterback grunt again and saw the football burst loose. At once the air was filled with hurtling bodies as first one player and then another dived for the tumbling football. It looked to Pete as if Gooberman was the one who finally covered the ball, and then the pile began to grow. A moment later—when they finally peeled off the last remaining player—Pete was pleased to see the monsterman curled happily about the football.

The game ended two minutes later with the score still the Canton Bulldogs 27, Potsdam 14.

As Pete clumped into the dressing room, he found it difficult to share his teammates boisterous enthusiasm. Yes, they had won their first game of the season—and had won decisively. Furthermore, that last defensive play of his had been very satisfying, indeed. In fact, his back was already beginning to protest the many hearty slaps it was getting from jubilant teammates. Nevertheless, Pete could still not rid himself of a nagging doubt concerning his effectiveness as a middle linebacker. He had made some good plays, sure. But twice he had missed sure tackles, he had been mousetrapped, and once he had tackled the wrong player.

Shaking his head, he slumped down in front of his locker and pulled off his jersey. Middle linebacking was not for him. Tackle. Left tackle. That was his position.

He stood up to unlace his shoulder pads and saw Frenchy Wells swing into the dressing room on a pair of crutches, a grim smile on his swarthy face, a thick bandage around his right ankle. When he caught Pete's eye, he smiled and swung over to him.

"You did pretty fair," he said. "Looks like you've got the job."

"What do you mean?" Pete demanded. "You've just got a sprained ankle, haven't you?"

Frenchy shook his head. "Doc Bender says that a broken bone is in there somewhere. I'll be on my way to the hospital in a couple of minutes for a cast. I'll be out for a month anyway. Isn't that something? And just a week before the Junior Prom."

Pete nodded. But he wasn't thinking of the prom. "The coach'll put someone else in at middle linebacker," he said. "I'd rather stay on the line."

Just then Coach Summers appeared in the doorway and beckoned to Frenchy.

"Well, here I go for my ride to the hospital," Frenchy said as he swung away from Pete.

"Stay loose," Pete called.

After a few words with Frenchy, Summers patted him on the back and sent him on his way. Then the coach walked over to Pete. Bill Summers was an assistant coach who handled mostly the team's defense.

"Nice going, Pete," the man said. "Looks like you're our new middle linebacker."

"I'd rather stay at tackle."

"Why?"

"I just would, that's all."

"You'll do fine at linebacker—until Frenchy's ankle clears up. I'm not worried, so why should you be?"

"I'm used to left tackle."

"You want me to put Tom Walton in at middle linebacker?"

"Is that all you've got?"

"That's all."

Pete considered a moment. Tom Walton was a nice kid and growing fast. But he was only a sophomore and didn't have the savvy—nor the heft—for middle linebacker. "All right, coach. But I'll need help. Frenchy's shoes are going to be hard to fill."

Summers's pleasant face sobered instantly. "I know that, Pete. You seem to have a little trouble with open field tackling, but you'll get all the help you need. I promise you."

"Thanks, coach."

"But don't worry. You did fine out there today." He slapped Pete on the back and moved off.

Pete watched him go. The coach was a shrewd one, all right. He'd caught those missed tackles—and all the rest of it—but he wasn't going to let that stop him from using Pete as a middle linebacker.

But then, what choice did he have?

Pete took a towel and a bar of soap from his locker and headed for the showers. He knew he was a worrier—and he was worrying overtime now. But he didn't really have any reason to worry. He was the new middle linebacker, and with the coach's help he was going to be a good one.

A moment later he was beginning to whistle as he walked through the billowing clouds of steam into the shower stalls.

Chapter Two

IT WAS CLOSE to five o'clock when Pete left the field house and started across the grass toward the parking lot behind the high school. There was still considerable light in the sky, and a fresh breeze was blowing with enough force to raise his damp hair slightly.

He was tired, deliciously so, the way it always was after he had given everything he had, never letting up for an instant, putting out one hundred percent for the full forty-eight minutes. There were specific muscles of his body—around the thighs and shoulders, especially—that ached with slightly more intensity than the rest of him, and his right calf was really sore. Though he couldn't remember being hit there, undoubtedly during one of the game's innumerable pileups, someone had come down hard on his exposed leg.

But it wasn't serious. Not at all. It was really only after games like this—when it seemed almost every muscle, every tendon, every nerve tingled with a life of its own—that he felt he was really alive; and he knew he would never forget these precious fall days when the sun grew colder, the sky bluer, and the sounds of a football game carried far.

He caught sight of Sandra waiting for him behind the wheel of her convertible and waved to her. The cream convertible went well with Sandra's long, dark hair. There was a dimple in her chin, and she had large, dark eyes.

Sandra Peters was her full name, and her father was perhaps the wealthiest man in town. He owned the paper mill out on the Norwood Road, two restaurants in town, and a hardware store. Sandra wanted for nothing and looked it. Her clothes were always the finest, and her cars the latest model of the current year. In her four years of high school, she had owned three different convertibles. The car she was sitting in now was her latest.

Of course it had not been easy—letting her drive him everywhere, and he was sure that the fact of her wealth was what made him feel somewhat uncomfortable with her at times. But she had a good heart and seemed to take his moods in stride. And he liked the way she stood up to him. She had a mind of her own and wasn't afraid to speak up. If only she would wear her hair in pigtails once in a while or learn to jump over fences—or something. She was always so immaculate, so cool and unruffled.

"You look happy," she said.

He smiled. "We won."

"Yes, so you did. Isn't it going to get a little boring this season? Winning all the time?"

"It isn't winning," he said with a grin as he got in beside her. "It's playing the game that counts."

"I thought it was the *way* you play the game that counts," Sandra said, starting the car.

Pete leaned back luxuriously, pressing down upon the deep, leather-covered cushions of the seat. "You heard right. It's playing the game that counts. And playing hard. That's what I love."

"And winning," she suggested, piloting the car out of the lot and turning onto Willow Street.

"Sure. And winning."

"Well, you won today. And you did fine."

He glanced quickly at her. "You went to the game?"

"That's right."

"How come?"

"I wanted to see you play today. I don't know why." She smiled at him. "I just did, that's all."

"Well, that's great—a real breakthrough, I'd say."

"Yes, I guess it is, at that."

It was a great deal for him to take in all at once. He looked out the window at the houses and trees and parked cars slipping past and felt a sudden wariness. All last season she had refused to attend any of Canton's games. There were more important activities in life, she had maintained, than carrying a football up and down a football field. This unwillingness on her part to join with him in his enthusiasm for a game that did so much to fill his life had been a constant source of friction between them. Now, suddenly, why the change of heart?

"Heard from Patty?" Sandra asked.

"Yeah, last Wednesday as a matter of fact."

"How does she like Ohio?"

"Just fine, so far. But she's lonely, of course."

"Well, it was a promotion her father really couldn't afford to pass up. But I guess it will be rough for a while until she makes new friends."

"You know Patty. It takes a lot to faze her. She'll have plenty of friends before long."

"Do you miss her?"

Sandra was turning onto Washington Street, where Pete lived. Sandra had asked the question casually, just as she had made the turn. But Pete knew it was not a casual question.

"Sure," he said. "I miss her."

She nodded and pulled up in front of his house, a

small, dark-brown shingled house with white trim, the trim bright and new. Pete's father had just finished repainting the trim only a few weeks before. A heaviness fell over Pete's spirits.

Sandra leaned over the seat as he got out of the car. "How's your father?"

"He's up and about now," he replied, pausing. "But I guess he'll never climb any more ladders for the light company."

"That's too bad, Pete. Is there anything I can do?"

"Thanks, Sandra. If there is, I'll let you know."

He closed the door firmly and stepped back as she drove off. Then he turned and went inside.

The brace his father was wearing made it difficult for the man to turn, but he did so as Pete walked out onto the back patio.

"You won," he said, smiling. "I heard it on the radio. Seems like you dumped the quarterback."

Pete smiled. "I'm now the team's middle linebacker."

"How come?"

Pete sat down in the lawn chair next to his father. "Frenchy Wells broke a bone in his ankle."

"I see. Well, how do you like playing linebacker?"

"It'll take some adjusting, I imagine." Pete said nothing more, aware again of a faint twinge of uneasiness as he recalled those two missed tackles and the rest of it.

"Adjusting . . . yes," Pete's father said, getting slowly, carefully to his feet.

Pete watched the man move cautiously across the patio. His father had always been a tall, craggy-faced individual who loved to move about and climb. As a crew chief at the local power and light company he had always prided himself on being the first one up a ladder.

"How's the back, Dad?"

Mr. Dennis stopped and turned, slowly. "Fine, just fine. I got word from the company today. They want me back as soon as I feel up to it."

"Hey, that's great, Dad."

"They want me back to pilot a desk. Dispatcher. I told them I won't do it. I'm not a cripple."

Pete didn't know what to say. "Of course you're not, Dad."

Mr. Dennis looked for a long moment at Pete, as if he were trying to ascertain whether or not his son was sincere. Then, his long, angular face softening not a bit, he nodded, turned, and started for the door.

"Dad . . . ?"

The man stopped again. "What is it?" he asked wearily without turning around.

"Sandra said if there were anything she could do, she'd be glad to help. And I was thinking. Her father has those two big plants . . ."

Pete's voice trailed off as his father turned laboriously and fixed Pete with his eyes. There was a moment or two of silence before Mr. Dennis replied.

"I don't need any help from your rich girl friend, Pete." He considered his son for a moment. "Are you going to go with Sandra again—now that Patty's gone?"

"I never really stopped seeing Sandra, Dad."

He nodded bleakly. "Well, I'll not be needing her help or her father's help if you don't mind."

He turned around again, and this time Pete let him go on into the house. A second or two later his mother appeared in the doorway.

"How long have you been home, Pete?"

"Just got in."

Her small round face brightened as she took a letter from her pocket. "A letter came for you today. It's from Patty, I think."

"Hey, great."

He took it from her and tore open the envelope, then looked back at his mother. She smiled and started back into the house.

"I've got to start supper," she said.

Pete took the letter over to the lawn chair and sat down.

Dear Pete,

I was terribly sorry to hear about your father. Frank wrote me all about it. It must have been a terrible fall he took, and I guess you are all just grateful he didn't injure himself more seriously, though of course a back injury is not anything to take lightly, especially for anyone as active as your father. Anyway, I'm glad he's going to be all right.

I guess you've already won your opener by now. I honestly think Canton will have an unbeaten season this year. Frank is sure of it, and so am I. I certainly do wish that I could be there to cheer you fellows on. Frank says if you do get into the conference play-off, he's going to drive up and get me. It's a long drive, but I'd really love to make it, so I'm hoping you guys really play football this season.

Write again, Pete. You're such a terrible correspondent, but I love to hear from you. I miss you and your folks very much. Be sure to give my love to them both. I sure do miss climbing over that wonderful back fence of yours and beating the daylights out of you at ping pong. Oh, I almost forgot. I'm now a cheerleader at my new high school. But you should see the school colors. They're simply awful—green and blue with yellow stockings and a yellow stripe! Ugh!

Well, so long. Write your old neighbor!

Love,
Patty

Pete read the letter over twice, searching for something in it that wasn't there and wincing at every mention of Frank Gooberman, her old steady and Pete's teammate. At last he folded it and went inside.

"Patty sends her love," he said to his mother.

She looked up from the potatoes she was peeling. "That's nice. Next time you write, you tell her how much we all miss her."

Pete nodded. "Where's Dad?"

She looked back down at the bowl of potatoes, selected one, and began to peel it, swiftly, expertly. "He's upstairs in his room."

"He's pretty upset, isn't he."

"Yes, he is, Pete."

She kept her head bent over the bowl of potatoes as if her life depended on her being able to get this one potato peeled in record time. He put his arms around her. She turned quickly and buried her face in his shoulder. He felt her little shoulders trembling as she began to cry softly. He waited patiently, saying nothing—knowing there was nothing he could say. After a while she pushed herself gently away, wiped her eyes with a few deft motions, and went back to her peeling.

"You go on up and rest a bit, Pete. I know how you always feel after a game. Supper will be ready in about an hour."

"We won, Mom."

She looked back at him. Her eyes were still a little red, but her smile was bright. "Fine, Pete. That's just fine."

As Pete went up the stairs to his room, he felt only weariness. Yes, he really needed a rest. And that was funny because he'd felt so great after the game.

But then life wasn't all a football game—as Sandra never tired of telling him.

Chapter Three

FOR THEIR SECOND game of the season, Canton was to play the Clayton Hawks on a Friday night in Clayton's new Municipal Stadium. That Friday evening eleven busses packed with students, cheerleaders, and most of the players pulled out of the Canton High parking lot a little after 6:30 and headed out of town for Clayton. A full hour and a half before game time, a steady stream of cars began to flow into Clayton, all of them turning down Main Street and heading directly for the new stadium. It looked as if the whole county was attending this game.

Sandra drove Pete, who along with Gooberman, Gary West, and a few others, had obtained permission from head coach Quenton to drive to the game in private cars.

Sandra and Pete were a few miles outside of Clayton when the conversation turned finally to Pete's father. Sandra asked how he was.

"He's all right."

"I meant what I said before, Pete. About helping out, I mean. I spoke to Dad about it last night. He knows what a responsible position your father held at the light company. He was a crew foreman, right?"

"Yes."

"Well, that's certainly a recommendation then. Dad has done some inquiries at the light company, and he's been very impressed with what he has found. He'd love to have a man with your father's qualifications in his Canton plant."

"Dad doesn't know anything about making paper."

"He could learn easily enough."

"He likes to work outside. He would hate to work inside a factory all day."

Sandra said nothing more. Pete had not looked at her once during the conversation. Now he did so.

"Thanks anyway, Sandra. I've got the feeling Dad's got to wrestle this one out all by himself. He's not much fun anymore, and every time I see him try to move around in that back brace I want to cry. But I guess right now the only way he feels he can show his independence is by refusing to take any help he doesn't ask for." Pete shrugged. "I guess I can understand that."

Sandra nodded. "Okay, Pete."

"So thanks again."

They were driving down Clayton's Main Street past the Clayton National Bank building. There was a big clock out front on top of a tall column, and Pete felt a tightening in his stomach when he saw what time it was. Clayton was going to be a difficult team for them to beat, and yet everyone was taking it for granted that they were going to win. But no one on the Canton team, from the coaches on down, were taking this game lightly. Clayton had a fine passer and a powerful fullback, along with an offensive line that was almost completely intact from last season. And last season they had finished only one game behind Canton in the conference.

Pete looked at Sandra. "This is really going to be a tough game for us."

Her eyebrows went up a notch. "Oh? I thought this was going to be just another notch in your belts—one more victory in the string you are about to fashion this season."

"That's what everybody thinks, I guess. Patty mentioned it in her letter. She said Gooberman was sure we were going to have an unbeaten season, and she's planning to be on hand for the conference playoffs."

"She is?"

"That's right." He glanced at her, aware suddenly of an edge in her voice.

"You do keep writing to her, don't you, Pete." It was not a question, but a statement.

"Of course."

She was silent for a while. Then she glanced coldly across the seat at him. "Pete, can you get a ride home tonight after the game?"

She meant, of course, with someone else, and this was not at all what he had intended. Moreover, he was sure that until this moment—until his mention of his correspondence with Patty—it was not what she had had in mind either.

"Sure. I can get another ride," he told her.

"I'd like to do some shopping while I'm here, Pete. They've got some good stores that stay open late. If I hurry I can get there before closing time, and then I'll get on back home. Okay?"

"No sweat, Sandra. I can probably get a ride with Gooberman or take the bus back."

They were pulling into the parking lot behind the stadium. Sandra made no effort to find a parking space. She just drove up to the players' entrance and let him off.

Both teams scored touchdowns in the first period, and each managed to kick their point after. In the second period Canton ground out two touchdowns, Kowalski doing most of the work, including a long punt return that put them on the Clayton twenty. Then the Canton defense tried, without success, to stem a determined march upfield by the Hawks that gave Clayton their second touchdown just before the close of the first half, making it 21 to 14.

The fans had expected a wide-open game, and they were getting it.

The Canton locker room was quiet, except for the deep breathing of the players slumped forward on the benches in front of their lockers, their elbows resting on their knees, their helmets off, their thick, tousled hair gleaming with perspiration. Paul Tompkins, the team manager, was passing slowly in front of each player, handing out paper cups filled with juice.

Quenton and Summers entered the locker room. Every face looked up, and every pair of eyes watched as the two coaches crossed the room and positioned themselves in front of the blackboard.

"No need to go over our offense," said Quenton. "Our game plan still looks pretty good so far. But our defense has me worried. Clayton didn't seem to have enough difficulty marching seventy-five yards on ten plays just before the half ended. Tighten up, defense. Especially down the middle."

Quenton turned to Summers. "Bill, I'll let you take it from here."

Summers nodded and stepped forward.

"All I can tell you guys is to move faster off that ball on the line. They're outcharging you. That means they've got the momentum. On the other hand," and here he smiled at the seeming contradiction of what he was about to say, "don't be too anxious." He was looking at Pete now. "Don't rush in so recklessly that they get to count on it."

"You mean me?" Pete asked.

The man smiled to take the sting out. "Yes, Pete. You're still thinking like a hard-charging lineman. Wait to see where the ball's going before you commit yourself."

Pete nodded. That was not exactly news to him. But what had been happening out there in the first period and most noticeably in the final quarter caused him to nod intently as Summers spoke.

Summers said nothing more to Pete directly and went on to an appraisal of the Clayton offense. Since they hadn't tried to go outside too often in the first half, Summers was pretty sure they didn't have the speed in their backs to do so. But he was worried about the quarterback's short passes—to his tight end particularly.

Then it was time to go, and as Pete got to his feet, he noticed that his usual eagerness to go out and really mix it up had given way to an unpleasant wariness—that of a fellow who had just been given a booby trap that hadn't yet gone off. But his uneasiness faded almost completely when West kicked a field goal to make the score 24 to 14.

Then lightning struck. A long pass—a desperation heave on the part of the Clayton quarterback—gave the Hawks a touchdown with only two minutes gone in the final period. A good rush, however, prevented Clayton's kick after from going through the uprights and kept the score 20 to 24.

There was no appreciable run back of the return kick, and Gary West was able to keep the ball for only six plays, after which he punted. The ball took a bad bounce and landed on the Clayton forty where a Hawk back gathered it in and knifed upfield to the Canton 45 before he was brought down.

Clayton now had less than six minutes to go, and they were down by a full touchdown, since a field goal would not tie it up. But that didn't seem to bother the Clayton fans. They were making so much noise that Pete had difficulty hearing the Clayton quarterback as he shouted out his signals.

On the snap the quarterback spun to his right, faked to his halfback coming around, then slipped the ball to his fullback in a dive up the middle. Pete had started through, caught the fake, and pulled back, just managing to fight clear of Clayton's center. The fullback's head was down, and he was pumping hard, already pulling free of one tackler's grasp when Pete met him waist high and buried his right shoulder into his midsection.

Pete felt himself being flung sideways, reached out and managed to grab the fullback's ankle as the back burst past him. The fullback's other foot came down hard on Pete's shoulder, and Pete felt himself being dragged over the ground. He yanked, stopped the fullback, and then reached up to grab his thigh. That was when Gooberman and the rest of the Canton tacklers plowed into the fullback.

The play was good for only two yards, and the clock was still running.

On second down the Hawk quarterback again faked to his halfback and gave the ball to his fullback up the middle—or so it appeared to Pete. Too late he realized his mistake as the fullback dived at him in an effort to cut him down.

Pete ducked wide and saw the quarterback, still with the ball, moving back into his pocket. Pete whirled. The tight end was streaking across the flat Pete had just vacated. Furious, Pete dug hard and flung himself at the end just as the fellow was reaching up for the ball. Pete hit him high and knocked him flat. But even before Pete stopped rolling, he knew that interference was going to be called. He had hit the end before the ball reached him.

Pete was right. First and ten on the Canton 35. Four minutes left.

"Never mind," said Gooberman. "You really nailed him. If he'd had the ball, he'd never have been able to hang on to it. Go for the ball now, Pete. Go for the ball. We've got to get it to stop these guys."

Pete nodded grimly and turned to wait for the Clayton huddle to break. If only he'd hit that end just a moment later—after he'd caught the ball. If. How many games had been lost on that one little word?

The Clayton huddle broke. Pete watched the quarterback closely. And suddenly he became certain that the fellow was going to pass. The quarterback seemed unusually eager, exhibiting a special alertness Pete was beginning to associate with a pass.

Should Pete blitz? He considered it only for an instant. If he blitzed, he'd again be leaving the hook zone open for that tight end.

But he was right. On the snap the quarterback took the ball straight back. Pete stood his ground a moment, then backed up as the slot back drifted through the line and then cut across the hook zone. The Canton front four were not able to break through the pocket, but the quarterback was not able to find anyone in the clear. He pumped once, held on to the ball, then broke out of his pocket.

The slot back was past Pete by this time, and Pete wanted that passer. He sprinted across the line toward the quarterback, who was all alone now as he headed for the sidelines, his arm back and ready to pass, his eyes searching downfield for an open receiver. As Pete got closer, he could almost feel the impact he was certain was coming.

Abruptly the quarterback stopped in his tracks and in one easy motion threw the ball, feather-soft, over Pete's head. Desperately, futilely, Pete reached up to knock the ball down. Then he spun about in time to see the slot back swoop in and catch the ball.

They didn't pull him down until he'd crossed the five-yard line.

There was a sick feeling in the pit of Pete's stomach as he waited for the next play to get under way. Clayton had stopped the clock with three minutes left to go.

The huddle broke. As the quarterback started for the line, he glanced once to his left and once to his right. He seemed wary, like a field general positioning his troops—not at all like a star about to dazzle the spectators.

No pass, Pete told himself grimly as the quarterback bent over his center and began to bark out the signals. On the snap the quarterback spun to his left and handed off to his halfback slanting over left end. The chunky halfback had just broken through when Pete plowed into him, driving him back and then slamming him decisively to the ground. Pete was a little woozy himself from the tackle, but the hearty slap on the back he received from Gooberman helped some.

Still second and five—now with less than two minutes to go.

"C'mon, gang," said Gooberman. "Hold 'em . . . and get that ball. Go for the ball!"

The players nodded, then went to their positions as the Clayton huddle broke. Again Pete watched the quarterback and noted his attitude. He was perky, alert, fairly tingling, his step light. Pete glanced quickly at Gooberman and formed the one word "pass" with his mouth. At once Gooberman indicated—with a barely perceptible nod in the direction of the quarterback—that Pete should blitz.

On the snap, Pete shot past the center. The quarterback was backpedaling frantically, but his pocket had not yet formed, and Pete was inside it anyway. The fellow saw Pete coming and tried to duck under his charge, but Pete kept low and hit the quarterback before he could spin away, catching hold of his jersey and spinning him roughly to the ground. Pete was hoping to shake loose the football, but the quarterback wrapped himself around the ball grimly and hung on to it as he bounced to the turf.

Third and eleven. Less than a minute to go with the clock still running.

The Clayton huddle broke. This time the quarterback was a field general. Pete braced himself for a play up the middle. On the snap, the quarterback faked the hand-off to the halfback cutting inside the guard, then flipped out to the fullback heading for the outside.

A sweep, the first one they'd tried in the second half!

Pete charged down the line, keeping pace with the fullback. Gooberman had broken through and was on the other side of the line just behind the fullback. And then abruptly Gooberman disappeared as he was cut down by a Clayton blocker. The back cut suddenly then for the corner of the end zone.

But Pete had a clear shot at him as he vaulted over a would-be blocker and lowered his shoulder. For just an instant he considered reaching out—but only for an instant. He wanted to knock this guy out of bounds. He flung himself, head down, like a human battering ram, but at that moment the back cut inside. Pete felt his shoulder graze the back's plunging thigh, then nothing as the back cleared him.

In a panic Pete reached out and tried to grapple the back to the ground. But it was too late as he struck the ground with numbing force and started to roll. He came to rest with his head on the out-of-bounds stripe. Dazedly, he looked back and was just in time to see the fullback slicing into the corner of the end zone.

The kick after was good: Clayton 27, Canton 24.

Not long after, Gary West was spinning frantically away from his pursuers in a desperate effort to get away one last pass. He was caught from behind; and as he sank beneath a storm of tacklers, the gun sounded, ending the game.

The locker room was like a funeral parlor. The players and the coaches moved about deliberately, quietly. No one slammed their locker doors. Those that spoke spoke softly, as if they were in the presence of a disaster so enormous that to speak of it aloud would surely bring the ceiling down upon their heads as a final, justifiable punishment.

No one stopped by Pete to tell him it was all right as he sat in front of his locker in his sweat-heavy T shirt and shorts. And Pete understood. They had lost, and it wasn't all right. They had failed. They had given it all they had, but it had not been enough. And Pete had failed as well. He'd missed tackles; he had guessed wrong on occasion, and each time it had cost, especially that time he'd tried to dump the quarterback. And though he'd made some nice plays as a linebacker, the sum of all his efforts had come out to a big fat zero.

He felt bone weary, and he knew the soreness, the aches would come later and would bother him more than usual—because they had lost. And he dreaded the ride back. He had already asked Gooberman and Frenchy Wells if he could go back with them, but he was not looking forward to it; the ride would be a long silent one as each one of them went over and over in his mind the whole futile effort.

Pete shook his head wearily, got up, and followed the silent line of players heading for the showers.

Chapter Four

PETE FLINCHED AND looked away from the game film. Frenchy Wells, sitting next to him, looked at Pete and rolled his eyes ceilingward and shrugged, as if to say, *There's nothing you can do about it now.*

Pete looked back at the small screen and tried not to wince. But it was not easy. Coach Quenton had gone back to the beginning of the final period, and everyone was being forced to sit through it a second time. Now, with the film's speed slowed to a dream-like pace, every poor pass, every half-hearted sprint after a ballcarrier became mercilessly apparent.

Numbly Pete watched himself charging along the line, saw himself vaulting a blocker, hesitate for just an instant—on the screen it was an instant that seemed to last forever—then, with agonizing slowness, lower his shoulder and fling himself futilely through the air at the ballcarrier, who was so obviously already past him.

Pete groaned softly and moved in his seat as he watched himself strike the back a glancing blow, then slowly bounce once . . . twice to the turf and just as slowly begin his turn to watch the ballcarrier.

"Don't take it so hard," Frenchy whispered. "Look at the bright side."

"The bright side?"

Frenchy grinned. "Sure. That wasn't me trying to make that tackle, and for that I'll be forever grateful."

The film ran out. Someone snapped the lights on while someone else pulled back the black curtains. Coach Quenton walked to the head of the classroom and stationed himself in front of the blank screen. The room became very quiet. Someone in the rear of the room cleared his throat nervously. The sound echoed as everyone waited for the blistering appraisal they all felt coming.

Quenton smiled.

"Okay," he said. "You guys have had enough punishment watching that film. Now let's get out onto that practice field and work ourselves back into something resembling a football team."

Pete was joining the stampede when he saw

Frenchy trying to keep up on his crutches. He slowed to allow Frenchy to keep pace with him.

"Never mind me, friend," said Frenchy. "You better get out there fast. I've got a feeling Summers wants to go over your open-field tackling some."

Frenchy was right. Summers put himself in charge of Pete's rather special workout, and standing on the sidelines with Pete and Frenchy, he began the session with an interesting comment.

"It is hard, deadly tackling," he said, "that is the greatest defensive weapon in this game. We coaches are always looking for fellows who can hit a ballcarrier and make it stick. But the thing is, Pete, you've got to hit them and hit them hard. And that means —on time. Remember that. Okay?"

Pete nodded somewhat bleakly. The implications of that last bit were not entirely lost on him. He turned and trotted out onto the field.

Summers began the session by sending the biggest players he could find at Pete. It was Pete's job to stop them and their job to get past him. At first a surprising number did just that.

After the fourth ballcarrier slammed through Pete, Summers walked out to talk to Pete. He didn't seem dismayed. Pete was, however.

"Look, Pete," Summers said. "Move in quickly—

a lot more quickly—and widen your base. Keep your head *up* and your eyes on the ballcarrier's midsection. Bend your knees a little more and keep your arms out in front of you—with the weight over the front knee."

Pete squinted up at him and nodded unhappily.

Summers shrugged and looked back to the sidelines at Frenchy. The former linebacker grinned at Pete and leaned forward on his crutches.

"He means spread your feet more," Frenchy shouted. "Keep your eye on the belt buckle and lean forward into the guy. Really *lean.*"

Summers smiled back at Pete. "Frenchy's got it. You understand now?"

"Sure. But I've *been* hitting them as hard as I can and leaning as far forward as I dare. And still they just keep right on going."

"Hit them harder. You're not hitting hard enough. As the ballcarrier gets to you, step forward and drive—really drive—your nearest shoulder into the fellow's middle or thigh. That's the secret. Really hit him hard, then shoot your head to one side and continue to move in close and wrap both arms around his legs. Keep going, but pull him *toward* you."

"Toward me?"

"That's right. Pull his legs toward you while at the same time you're driving the top of him back. Then lift him and dump him backward. If you've done it right, you'll end up spread-eagled over the guy with your shoulder still stuck in his middle."

"That's a lot to remember," Pete said, shaking his head.

Frenchy yelled. "Lean into him—hard—wrap him up and dump him!"

Summers laughed. "Frenchy's right. That's what I mean."

Then he turned and walked back to the sidelines.

Pete did a little better after that. As often as not, however, he'd stop the ballcarrier and end up under the fellow. It was only toward the end of the session that he began to dump his victims the way Summers wanted—with him ending up on top of them, his shoulder tucked snugly into a player's midsection.

When Pete left the gym for home, Frenchy was waiting outside for him. As he swung in beside Pete, he said, "Coach thinks I should cultivate your acquaintance more. He wants a little of my wit and wisdom to rub off on you. Think it's possible?"

"I doubt it," said Pete gloomily. "But we might as well give it a try."

"You can repay me right away," drawled Frenchy. "My car's over there, but I wish you'd drive. With this cast on, I'm a menace to navigation."

Pete looked down at the cast, astonished that

Frenchy would even attempt to drive with his foot so encumbered. "Sure. I'll be glad to drive."

Once they were under way, Pete glanced at Frenchy. "You don't seem to be suffering too much."

Frenchy was leaning back in the passenger seat, obviously enjoying his status as passenger. "Aha! You noticed."

"I noticed. But you've sure put me on the spot. Last season I had to learn how to play on the line. Now I'm a linebacker."

Frenchy raised his hands in mock horror. "So help me, Pete. I didn't do it on purpose. That's a fact."

Pete shrugged. "Well, I'm still on the spot."

"The griddle, friend. The griddle. And I can hear you sizzling from here. You seem to have a thing about open-field tackling. I think you're gun-shy, that's what I think."

"Thanks. Thanks a lot. That's the kind of encouragement I can really use." Pete took the next corner rather sharply.

"Hey," protested Frenchy as he grabbed for one of his crutches. "Don't take it personally. I haven't paid off this car yet, let alone the insurance." His face lost its grin, and he looked seriously across at Pete. "We all get gun-shy once in a while, Pete. It happens whenever we get run over by some mad fullback. But you'll get over it. We all do." He smiled suddenly and stretched luxuriously, or as luxuriously as his cast would allow. "Only now, with my current affliction, I don't have to worry about such neurotic concerns."

Pete laughed. He found himself liking Frenchy more every minute. He spoke the truth, but he knew how to mix it with a little humor. And it really helped. That was one thing he guessed he had been missing since Patty's departure—humor. He really needed to laugh more often. He had been getting a bit too grim lately.

"So breaking your ankle hasn't slowed you down any. That right?"

"Slowed me down? Just the opposite. By the way, I broke only a small bone. I should be out of this cast in about three weeks as good as new. But as for slowing me down—let me give you an idea; last week I was swinging along to my French III class in the annex when who do I see on the horizon—Mary Dolan." He glanced at Pete. "I hope you know of whom I speak, *the* Mary Dolan."

Pete was laughing. "Go on," he said. "I know Mary. She's very nice."

"All right. Well, for three long, lonely years now I've been hoping to catch that lovely's eye—but alas! All to no avail. This time, I vowed, things would be different."

"What did you do, hit her over the head with one of your crutches?"

"Not quite. But you're beginning to get the idea. What I did was drop my *History of the Western Republics,* my *Norton Anthology of Western Drama, Les Miserables,* my French book, two notebooks, a yellow pencil, a pen, and an eraser. Oh, the clatter it made! Makes me shudder now even to think of it."

"On purpose? You dropped all this on purpose?"

"Quite right, sir. This poor crippled football player suddenly lost all control and everything gave way. I suppose you can guess what happened after that."

"Let me think a minute. Oh, yes. Mary Dolan picked them all up for you."

"Precisely, my dear Dr. Watson. Not only did she pick them up for me, but she carried them for this poor crippled football player all the way to his next class. Meanwhile, of course, I engaged her mind, acquainted her with the brilliance of my repartee, obtained her phone number and the promise of a date. Last night was our third."

"A date? In that cast?"

"The cast is on my foot, friend. My arms are still nimble and free."

Pete laughed. "Where do you live? Johnson Avenue?"

Frenchy nodded. "It's not far from where you live."

"Why don't you come over to my place after supper? Maybe you can give me some more pointers about tackling."

"Sure. What time?"

"About seven-thirty."

"Okay."

"And Frenchy," Pete said as he turned down Johnson Avenue, "bring along that sense of humor, will you?"

Frenchy laughed. "It's a deal."

The moment Pete walked into the house, he sensed a difference—a lightness in the air. And then—from the kitchen—he heard Patty's laugh.

"Hey, Patty!" he called, hurrying down the front hall and into the kitchen.

"Pete!" she cried, throwing herself into his arms.

"What's the occasion? We haven't won the championship yet. What are you doing back in town?"

She looked him over. What she found evidently pleased her, because she wrinkled her nose and hugged him affectionately again.

"Hey, Mom," Pete cried, "hasn't she grown! Wow!" Then he looked back at her. "Come on, now. What are you doing back here?"

"It's the house," she replied. "Mom and Dad have decided to sell it outright to the Carters. They're offering us a fine price, so my folks are closing the deal tomorrow. I thought I'd just tag along and see my old buddies." She grinned at Pete. "And especially my big brother."

"Brother!"

"What's all the racket down here?"

Pete turned as his father loomed cautiously in the doorway, a broad smile on his face as he opened his arms to Patty.

She rushed into them and hugged Pete's father, but gently. For a moment the big man, his face wreathed in a smile, held his favorite neighbor's daughter in his arms and then released her. With considerable care Patty stepped away from him, anxious like all of them for his injured back.

As Pete looked at them, he remembered something his mother had said a year or so ago. *Your father wanted so badly to have had a daughter—someone like Patty.* It had really set Pete to thinking. And he was still thinking.

"How long are you going to be here, Patty?"

"Today, tomorrow, and the weekend—at least."

"Hey, that's great."

"It sure is! Goober's going to run me ragged!"

At mention of Frank Gooberman, things went a little sour for Pete all of a sudden. "Oh . . . Gooberman. I was hoping . . ."

But he didn't finish. Pete was never very good at hiding his feelings, and in that instant everyone in the kitchen seemed to be looking at Pete's face.

"I'm . . . sorry, Pete," said Patty. "I didn't think. I should have saved one evening for my favorite next-door neighbor, but your mom said you were still dating Sandra."

"Oh, that's all right, sport," said Pete, as carelessly as he could manage. "I'll survive."

Awkwardly he turned and started for the stairs at the end of the hall.

"Pete . . . !" Patty called.

He stopped and turned.

"Is there anything wrong," she asked, moving into the hallway after him, a concerned smile on her face.

At that moment he became overpoweringly aware of her light, still freckled complexion and the deep blue of her eyes.

"I was hoping," she said, "we could play a game of ping pong before supper."

"No. Nothing's wrong, Patty. But I just had a real tough workout on the practice field. I'm awful tired. Maybe after supper. Okay?"

"Oh, sure, Pete. Of course."

Pete turned and went on up the stairs. He *was* tired. Every muscle in his body was protesting. But when he threw himself down on his bed and closed his eyes, he found he was wide awake—his mind in a turmoil. Sleep was out of the question.

Instead, he found himself going over in his mind a visit he had made to the Naval recruiter the day before. The fellow's office occupied an old storefront across the street from the post office.

The petty officer looked very smart in his white naval uniform and had been very patient with Pete, obviously glad to answer any and all questions Pete might have.

"First of all, Pete," he said after they had introduced themselves. "Finish your high school education."

"I can get out in January if I want," Pete said.

"All right. But there's no hurry. Get as much as you can out of high school. The Navy doesn't want drop-outs."

Pete nodded. "I know that. I'm interested in the technical training program you're supposed to offer."

The officer smiled and leaned back. "That's what we like, Pete. Someone who's interested in the Navy for the educational challenge it offers. Have you any program in mind specifically?"

Pete picked up off the officer's desk a brochure he had been glancing through when he first came in. He handed it to the officer. "I like what this says about the Navy's nuclear program."

"Fine, Pete, but you must be eighteen. This program prepares for service aboard nuclear-powered submarines and surface ships. You'll broaden your scientific and technical background in all subjects related to such things as nuclear engineering as well as provide yourself with a pretty fine theoretical knowledge of the principle of atomic and nuclear physics and reactor engineering." He looked up and smiled quickly.

"Wow," said Pete.

"Interested?"

"I sure am. Reactor engineering. That's going to be the future in generating electricity."

The man nodded. "And desalinization plants too, probably. But there's one thing, Pete. To enter this program—and others comparable—you'll have to enlist in the Navy for four years and enter into an agreement to serve two more years."

"Six *years?*"

"Yes, Pete. Six years. Some college education combined with service. Seems like a long time, I'm sure. But it'll take that long for the Navy to get back its investment in your extensive training, Pete."

Pete had left then and walked home slowly, thinking it over. Six years was quite a slice out of a guy's life. Six years.

After reaching home, Pete fell across his bed. What would life in the Navy be like? Perhaps it would not be so bad after all.

Perhaps. . .

He closed his eyes and finally dropped off to sleep.

Later, during supper, Pete felt better as Patty's chatter gradually restored his sagging spirits. Pete's father benefited undoubtedly from Patty's presence. Once, at a remark of Patty's concerning her new history teacher, he put his head back and roared.

After supper when Patty reminded Pete of his promise to play her a game of ping pong, Pete offered no protest and went out onto the patio with her.

As the game progressed, he discovered that Patty had lost none of her deadly accuracy, and in fact seemed to have gained even more. Her serves came at him like deranged mothballs, and no matter how he slashed his returns to her, she could still—almost casually it seemed—return his ball with deft ease and slice it off a corner just beyond his reach.

In the middle of the second set, the phone rang. Pete paid no attention and slashed a return to the far corner. But Patty—apparently aware of the phone's ring—was momentarily slow in getting over. The ball flew past her lunging paddle.

Pete straightened. "That makes it eighteen to twenty. I'll catch up with you yet."

"Patty," said Pete's mother from the doorway, "you're wanted on the phone."

"Oh!"

Patty dropped her paddle and hurried inside. Pete followed to the doorway and watched her pick up the kitchen phone, her face aglow.

"Oh, hi, Frank!" she cried delightedly.

Pete turned and went back out onto the patio and picked up his paddle. After a few seconds he began batting the ball into the air. He soon tired of this and by the time Patty returned to the patio, he had to work hard to fight back a scowl, despite the glow on Patty's face. As they resumed the game, Pete found it difficult to regain his enthusiasm, and Patty quickly, deftly outpointed him to take it all.

"Thanks," said Patty, slapping her paddle down on the table. "Frank will be coming after me in a little while, Pete. I'll go in now and freshen up."

Pete nodded.

Patty started to say something, caught herself, then said, "Pete, we're like a sister and a brother. Okay?"

Pete shrugged, then found himself grinning. "Okay, Sis."

She registered a light kiss on his forehead as she flew past him. Pete shrugged and went inside.

Frenchy Wells came over about a half hour after Patty left with Frank and decided that—despite his crutches—he wanted a game of ping pong with Pete. It was a wild and zany game, full of impossible slams and lucky returns, with Frenchy wheeling about the patio on his crutches and Pete splitting his sides with laughter. The game ended when one of Frenchy's crutches caught a leg of the table and sent it crashing to the floor of the patio. Still, it was only with reluctance that Frenchy agreed to quit the game. He then decided that Pete should go bowling with him.

"Just tell me one thing," Pete said, as he started into the kitchen after Frenchy. "How are you going to bowl on crutches?"

"Very simple. I approach the line very swiftly on my trusty crutches, the bowling ball held securely in my teeth. At the right moment I drop the ball."

"Yeah. And destroy your other foot."

"Not so. But there *is* one catch."

"What's that?"

"I think to be fair, you should have to bowl backwards through your legs. It's not such a bad handicap. In fact, you might eventually prefer bowling that way."

Pete was reaching for his jacket, contemplating what next to say to this crazy new friend of his when he happened to glance into the living room. He paused in surprise at what he saw.

His father was sitting on the edge of the couch, looking with concern and a bit of puzzlement at what appeared to Pete to be a disassembled vacuum cleaner spread out before him on the rug. But it was not the family's own vacuum cleaner, one that Pete remembered as an old model. This was a modern cleaner, every gleaming piece like new.

"What's that you got there, Dad?" Pete asked, advancing into the living room.

"A vacuum cleaner."

"Oh, we bought a new one?"

"No," the man said grimly. "I'm going to sell them."

He looked up at Pete then and fixed him with an almost defiant stare—as if he were daring Pete to say anything.

But Pete kept his mouth buttoned shut and kept his response to a shrug.

"There's good money in this," his father said. "And it's work that will take me outside."

"Sure, Dad."

His father went back to a diagram he had been consulting earlier. Pete turned and left the room.

Once outside with Frenchy, he shook his head. "A vacuum cleaner salesman! Isn't that just great!"

"Now don't knock it," said Frenchy as he swung along beside Pete. "Like your father said, it's outside work. Besides, you get to meet such interesting people—irate housewives, furious husbands, and little kids with jam all over their faces."

"And don't forget the dogs," Pete reminded him. "The German shepherds are really enthusiastic." Pete shook his head. "How can I possibly joke about this? It doesn't seem like something Dad v

"Aw, c'mon, Pete. You're like an old

Your father can take care of himself." He looked at Pete. "You sound like a mother hen."

Yes, Pete realized. Just like a mother hen. What was the matter with him anyway? He ought to leave his father alone and let him do what he wanted. After all, a person had his own problems, not the least of which was the game coming up this next Wednesday. This thought sobered him—along with the memory of a conversation he had just had with the Navy recruiter at the post office yesterday.

But Pete was unable to stay gloomy for long with Frenchy swinging wildly along beside him. And soon he was beginning to believe that Frenchy would indeed approach the bowling lane with a bowling ball grasped securely in his teeth.

And he began looking forward to the experience of bowling backward through his legs!

Chapter Five

PETE HEARD THE cry, "Pass!" and turned. The ball was already in flight, heading directly over his head. The Tompkinsville right end, beyond him now in the flat, was reaching up.

But as the ball passed over, Pete leaped. For a split second he seemed to hang there, suspended. Then he felt the underside of the football as it just grazed his forefinger. He came down off-balance slightly. Someone hit him, and he went sprawling. But the ball had already veered to the left and was wobbling.

It was Gooberman who flashed over and caught the ball. Without breaking stride, he lit out down the sidelines. For a moment it looked as if he might go all the way, but the Tompkinsville quarterback nailed him finally on the twenty-five.

The Canton Bulldogs were playing the Tompkinsville Titans on the Canton home field, and as Gooberman neared the sidelines, the home crowd gave him a standing ovation.

Pete found a place on the bench beside Frenchy and sat down. "That's the way to go in there, Pete," Frenchy said.

"Sure. Sure."

"Too bad so few noticed you were the one who tapped that ball," Frenchy went on. "It looks like Gooberman's getting all the credit."

"Well, Patty's in the stands, you know. So it's just working out fine for the two of them."

The crowd's sudden roar brought Pete to his feet just in time to see Kowalski bowling over the last Titan player as he powered into the end zone.

The kick after was good, making the score Canton 14, Tompkinsville 7. Pete stood up and prepared to run back out onto the field.

"Lower that shoulder, Pete," Frenchy said. "Really hit hard now."

A few minutes later, as the Titan quarterback raced back into his pocket to pass, Pete—on a blitz—bowled past one of the Titan guards and reached out for his arm. The quarterback pulled it down and spun away. Someone hit Pete from the side, but he stayed on his feet and reached out again for the quarterback. Too late. The arm flashed forward, and the ball was on its way, a perfect spiral.

The Titan scatback was in the clear just beyond in the flat. He leaped, caught the ball, and kept going downfield. One quick sidestep and he was in the open, with no one between him and the goal line.

And then—seemingly out of nowhere—Gooberman pulled abreast of the back and cut into him from the side. Pete winced as he saw the scatback jacknife and slam into the ground, Gooberman on top.

A sudden cry from the crowd alerted Pete. And then he saw the football—evidently knocked loose from the force of Gooberman's tackle—skittering across the yard stripe. A storm of players streamed toward it, most of them wearing blue-and-white jerseys. A moment later the referee indicated that it was Canton's ball as he pulled it out of Paul Christman's sweaty grasp.

First and ten for Canton on their own five.

Gary West kept the ball on the ground for three plays and then punted from the seven. It was a great punt that rolled out of bounds on the Titan forty.

"Don't blitz, Pete," said Gooberman, leaning close. "Stay back to fill the holes."

Pete nodded, a little unhappily.

The Titan huddle broke. The quarterback approached the line, looked it over, then began barking out his signals. Pete itched to blast through, but kept the impulse in check and waited. On the snap the quarterback whirled and handed off to his fullback driving past him into the center of the line. Pete was bracing himself to stop the fullback when he heard Gooberman's shout.

"End around! End around!"

Glancing up, Pete saw the Titan halfback—the football tucked under his arm—slanting through a hole in the left side of the line. Pete turned to start after him, but that was when the fullback cut him down. Scrambling out from under the debris of arms and legs, Pete got back onto his feet just in time to see Gooberman overtake the halfback and knock him out of bounds close to the Canton forty-five.

Pete shook his head ruefully as he joined the defensive huddle. "I was waiting for the fullback," he said. "I thought *he* had the ball."

"That quarterback is a great faker, Pete. You've just got to watch him a little closer." Gooberman grinned. "Besides, I remembered that play from last year."

On the next play Gooberman blitzed from the left side and sent the quarterback reeling to the ground with a fourteen-yard loss. The quarterback got up slowly. On the next play, the quarterback handed off quickly to his fullback for a plunge up the middle. This time Pete was waiting and dumped him.

"Third and twenty-four," Gooberman told the huddle. "He'll fake something and pass. Pete, stay back. I'll blitz."

Gooberman called it perfectly. The quarterback faked a plunge, then jumped and let fly. The right end slanted just in front of Pete, reached back and took the ball in stride. As he was tucking it away, Pete hit him—as hard as he could, ramming his shoulder into the fellow's right side and driving with all the force he could generate. He heard the end gasp as he slammed to the ground on top of him. The ball popped loose. Pete reached out for it, got a hand on it, then lost it. On his hands and knees he scrambled frantically after it, only to have it booted away as a storm of players descended on the elusive pigskin.

It was Gooberman who recovered the fumble.

The game ended five minutes later with Gary West kicking a field goal to make it 17 to 7.

The locker room was quiet as the players began to gather around Gooberman's locker. Almost as if everyone had thought of it at the same time, there was a general unspoken consensus that Gooberman should be given a game ball. As Pete joined the crowd, Gomer Peterson thrust a football at him.

"Here, you give it to him," said Gomer.

Pete pushed through those closest to Gooberman and handed the football to him. Gooberman took it and swallowed. Since the practice of giving game footballs to players who distinguished themselves in an individual game was not a habit with the Canton team, Gooberman was at a loss. He swallowed a second time.

"Speech!" someone yelled at him from the back.

"I owe it all to my breakfast cereal!" Gooberman said with a sudden smile. He held the football up and stared idiotically at an imaginary camera.

The locker room shook with cheers.

Pete slapped Gooberman on the back, then returned to his locker and started to climb out of his suit. A moment later, on his way to the shower, Frenchy swung by.

"Cereal, my eye," Frenchy said. "He knew Patty was in the stands. A girl friend can do wonders for a guy's morale."

As Pete pulled his jersey over his head, he smiled ironically to himself. Had Sandra been in the stands?

"Hey, you two. Want a ride?"

Pete and Frenchy turned to see Gooberman pulling up beside them in his convertible, Patty snuggled beside him on the front seat.

"Sure," said Frenchy.

As they got under way, Patty twisted around in the front seat and smiled at them. "Boy, Pete, that was some game, huh?"

"Yes, it sure was."

"If you mean didn't Gooberman do just great," said Frenchy with a smile, "the answer I suppose has to be 'yes'."

"That's *just* what I meant."

"Hey, you guys! Cut it out, will you?" Gooberman pleaded. "Enough is enough."

"Where's the game football?" Pete asked.

"In the trunk. Boy, you guys really embarrassed me."

Patty laughed, her head kicking back. "You know what? He's going to enshrine that ball."

"Patty!" Gooberman cried.

"And I think that's a fine idea. You were great," Patty said. "And *I* know why."

"Sure. And *I* know why too," said Pete.

Patty was suddenly alert. "You know why?"

"That's right," said Frenchy. "He ate his breakfast cereal."

Patty smiled at Gooberman. "Is *that* what you told them?"

Gooberman smiled back at her and nodded.

Patty laughed. And in that instant Pete felt his heart dip. He knew at once why Gooberman had played so well, and it wasn't entirely the fact that Patty was in the stands—it was something more.

"Patty?" he asked, his voice sounding kind of hollow. "When are you going back to Ohio?"

Patty glanced quickly at Gooberman. He winked back at her. She looked at Pete."I'm not, Pete. I'm staying at your house until graduation. I want to finish high school at Canton High, and your mother and father talked to my parents, so I'm boarding here."

"Also," Gooberman said, "Patty and I are going steady again."

"Oh," was all Pete could manage.

"Hey, that's great!" cried Frenchy.

Pete kept the chatter light after that, in keeping with Frenchy's fine irreverence, and he still had his smile pasted on when he climbed out of the car over Frenchy's crutches a few moments later.

As soon as Gooberman drove off, his smile vanished. Well, he thought, turning to start up the walk. That's that.

His father was standing in the front hall, slowly pulling on his coat. Beside him on the rug was a vacuum cleaner, a deluxe model.

"Getting an early start," the man told Pete. "Best

time to sell is when both the husband and wife are home."

Pete stopped. "That means you'll be working nights a lot."

"Evenings, Pete. But only for about four hours or so. I'm not supposed to make any house calls after nine. And I make some calls during the day to set up appointments."

He stood there looking at Pete, seemingly reluctant to get moving.

"Where's your first appointment tonight?" Pete asked.

"Jack Johnson and his wife. I worked with Jack at the light company. He retired a couple of years ago."

Pete nodded.

"I called them up this afternoon. They said their own vacuum cleaner is pretty old."

Again Pete nodded.

"Well, I guess I'd better get going."

He reached down carefully and picked up the vacuum cleaner and started for the door. As Pete watched, he realized it was more than his aching back that caused him to move so slowly.

When the door closed behind him, Pete's mother appeared in the kitchen doorway. "Is he gone?" she asked.

Pete nodded.

She sighed. "I do hope he likes it, but . . ." She shook her head and turned back into the kitchen.

Pete followed after her and sat down at the table, watching her busy herself cleaning the stove. He was about to ask her about Patty, but thought better of it. She was obviously in no mood to discuss Patty right now.

She took a sponge and wiped over the top of the stove. Although it was already shining, she began wiping the chrome around the burners with a paper towel. "He's been practicing his sales speech all afternoon," she said without looking at Pete. "And no matter how hard he tries, he keeps getting it all mixed up." She turned suddenly to Pete. "He hates it, Pete. I can tell. And, Pete, he's not made more than a few dollars this past week—just enough to pay for his sample kit and all the literature he's supposed to pass out. We're eating into our life savings, Pete—and that means what we've been saving for you, for college."

It was about what Pete had figured. This was why he'd gone in to speak to the Naval recruiter. With his father out of work, a good technology college was out of the question. But the Navy, according to what the recruiter had told Pete, did put quite a bit of emphasis on technical training.

"Pete, what are we going to do?" his mother asked.

"Don't worry, Mom; I know Dad is going to work something out.

"Are you and Sandra seeing each other now?" his mother asked changing the subject.

Pete hesitated a moment before answering. "I was

just thinking about calling her," Pete said, realizing at that moment that he'd been waiting for an excuse . . . "In fact, I think I'll go do that right now."

He got up and went to the hall phone and dialed Sandra's number.

Sandra's mother answered. She seemed pleased to hear Pete's voice. Yes, Sandra was in. She asked him to hold on.

Pete waited a considerable time, and then a very flustered Mrs. Peters took up the phone. "I'm terribly sorry, Pete," she said. "I thought Sandra was in—but she's gone out. "I'll—I'll tell her you called."

"That's all right, Mrs. Peters," Pete said. "I understand."

He hung up and stood there a moment, then shrugged and went back into the kitchen.

Chapter Six

PETE LUNGED. GOMPSON straight-armed him and dodged aside. Pete attempted to reach around his teammate's plunging thighs and grapple him more securely. But the fellow kept driving, and Pete felt himself turning completely around. Suddenly he was just hanging onto Gompson's thigh—going along for the ride.

Gompson lifted his knees high and lunged forward. Pete let go. For a moment he lay on the turf, watching the husky sophomore race a few yards farther down the field before turning back. Then he got wearily, disgustedly to his feet.

"Next victim!" Summers cried from the sideline.

Someone tossed Kowalski a football. He caught it

casually in his enormous hands, grinned over at Pete, and started to trot happily in his direction.

Pete planted himself, leaned far forward, and waited. At the last minute Kowalski veered. Pete followed him and dived, driving his nearest shoulder deep into Kowalski's side, just under the ribs. Kowalski gasped. Pete flung both arms around the big fullback and started to pull him toward him as he kept driving at Kowalski from the side. He felt the big fullback stumble. It gave him great satisfaction, and he redoubled his efforts to bring the boy down.

Kowalski kept his balance, however, and tried to spin Pete off. Pete felt the enormous weight of Kowalski's right hand chopping down onto his shoulder. Pete winced and hung on, dug his feet in, and drove his head into the fullback's side with redoubled fury. Kowalski gasped and went down with such a crunch that the ball popped loose.

"Nice going, Pete!" called Frenchy.

Pete got slowly to his feet, aware of the stares of more than one scrimmaging ballplayer. In fact, everyone it seemed had been watching him during this whole miserable workout.

Kowalski rolled over and looked up at Pete. "Well, anyway, I made it tough for you, Pete. You know what they say about old Kowalski—the lucky ones fall off."

"I guess I wasn't lucky," said Pete.

He turned then and started off the field. It was late. Past five. And they had been out there since three. He was tired. And humiliated. Just because the last game had been all Gooberman's didn't mean he hadn't done anything. Anyway, he was sick of the whole business. On the line he had been all right. But this linebacking. Well, this was something else again. And all this switching around. He had started last season as the fullback. Then he had had to go into the defensive line. Now linebacker.

He didn't need it. He really didn't. Frenchy's cast was due to come off this week—and then Frenchy could have the middle linebacking spot all to himself. Pete had had it. Right up to here!

"Where you going, Pete?" asked Coach Summers as Pete continued on past him.

"The locker room. I'm through."

"What's the matter?"

Pete just kept on walking. He didn't trust himself to speak.

He showered quickly and walked home. By the time he got there, he had walked off most of the steam that had been building constantly during the afternoon's practice, but he still felt rather grim.

"Is that you, Pete?"

It was his mother sitting on the sofa in the living

room. He went in. She was looking down at his father's vacuum cleaner—or rather its pieces. They were scattered in gleaming random all over the rug.

"What's wrong, Mom?"

She looked up at Pete and smiled. But the smile was an effort. "Your father's home. He just came in without a word and dumped all this over the rug. Then he turned and stormed upstairs to his room. When he slammed the door, the whole house shook."

"No sales, I guess. Boy, this must be a pretty tough job."

"I think it's more than that, Pete. But I don't know what it is. And he left here this afternoon so full of enthusiasm!" She shook her head. "He even gave me some idea of how much he might clear this week. And he seemed so pleased with himself. Oh, Pete, if only he'd go back to the light company—something steady. All this tramping around, carrying a heavy vacuum cleaner."

"Cheer up, Mom. Dad'll come out of it. Don't worry."

She looked at Pete for a long moment, appeared visibly to pull herself together, then nodded sharply and smiled. "You're right, Pete. I shouldn't go on like this. I don't know what's got into me. Are you hungry?"

"I could eat a horse."

She smiled, got up, and headed for the kitchen. "One horse, coming up."

As soon as she had disappeared into the kitchen, Pete went upstairs into his room and sat on the edge of his cot. He could hear his mother preparing the supper below him in the kitchen, and he knew that just down the hall from his room his father was sitting grimly in his office, pondering what to do next.

Pete wondered if he should go in to see his father and cheer him up. He had never tried anything like that before. It was not that they did not get along. Pete would never cross his father, mostly because the man gave him all kinds of freedom, so that when he did set a limit, Pete understood there was a good reason for it.

Yet, although they lived in the same house without conflict, it was without any real closeness either. They ate at the same table, they chatted about football, but that was the extent of their involvement in each other's personalities. It seemed to Pete—and this came to him now with sudden sharpness as he sat on his cot—that he had never really known his father when the man wasn't being his father—a powerful figure who laid down the law and brought home the bacon, a silent, proud man that Pete respected greatly . . .but wanted to love.

What must he be thinking now? Pete wondered. Always, until now, his father had been on top of every situation, a strong man commanding the respect of all. Now he was reduced to peddling vacuum cleaners door to door and having a difficult time of it. Perhaps this very day a dog had chased him . . . a little mutt perhaps, yipping and snarling at his heels. Maybe a busy housewife had slammed a door in his face, and he had had to swallow his anger and turn quietly and go back down the porch steps.

Pete took a deep breath and stood up, squared his shoulders and left the room. He paused only a second in front of his father's office, then knocked.

"Come in," called his father.

Pete pushed the door open and walked in. His father was sitting at his desk, his back to the window. In front of him on the blotter lay his kit and the text of his sales pitch. He had obviously been studying it when Pete knocked.

"Hi, Dad. What's up?"

He looked bleakly at Pete. "I guess I am."

"What's wrong?"

Pete closed the door and sat down in a chair by his father's desk.

The man sighed and leaned back in his chair. "This door-to-door selling, Pete. It's not exactly my meat, if you know what I mean."

"Is it the dogs?"

His father smiled. "That's right, Pete. The dogs. And the tired, weary housewives too busy to give you any time. And the unhappy husbands who force themselves to listen to my sales pitch when they'd much rather be watching their favorite TV program."

Pete nodded glumly. "Well, you'll get used to it, Dad."

His father scratched his head and thought a moment. "Well, there *are* some fellows who make a bundle selling these vacuum cleaners." He laughed shortly and shook his head in wonder. "In fact, there's one guy in Cleveland who makes over one thousand a month."

"Wow!"

"But that's not me, Pete. I can just imagine how he operates. He must use a sledgehammer."

"Still, you *have* been selling, Dad. Didn't you sell two vacuum cleaners last week?"

"That's right. I sold a couple." He smiled ruefully. "Two friends of mine felt sorry for me, Pete. They bought vacuum cleaners off me just to help me out."

"Are you *sure* that's why?"

The man nodded glumly. "I'm sure. Didn't take much brains to figure it out. A friend of mine called me up this morning and suggested that his own vacuum cleaner was getting old. He said Bill Forman—that's one of the fellows I sold one to last week—had suggested he give me a call, that I might appreciate the business."

He looked at Pete and frowned sadly. Pete looked away. There was no sense in trying to deny it. What was happening was perfectly clear all right. His father had a lot of friends. They wanted to help. And this was how they figured they could do it.

"So you see, Pete?"

"Sure, Dad. Maybe you're right. But all it really means is you've got some really great friends."

He smiled. "Thanks, Pete. It does mean that, doesn't it. And yet how long do you think I'll keep my friends if I let them do this sort of thing for me?"

Pete could see the truth in that. He thought a moment. "So what now?"

"That's just what I've been sitting here trying to figure."

"What about that job at the light company?"

"It's no longer available. They held it for me as long as they could."

"Oh, I'm sorry, Dad."

"Thanks, Pete. But it's my own fault, and now I'm stuck with this job." He looked back at the sales pitch on his desk. "I guess what I have to do is really rather simple at that. I have to buckle down and learn how to sell vacuum cleaners. I'll have to memorize this darn sales pitch once and for all and stop counting on my friends. From now on I'll talk only to people who don't know me."

He looked at Pete for a long moment, then abruptly stood up. "But first," he said with a sudden smile, "I'm going downstairs and talk to your mother. I must have upset her the way I came in a little while ago."

"Okay, Dad," Pete said as he got up and opened the door.

"Pete . . .?"

Pete turned.

"Thanks. Thanks a lot."

"What for?"

"For coming in here like this. I really appreciate it."

Pete felt himself blush. "Oh, that's all right, Dad."

"Do me a favor, will you, Pete?"

"Sure, Dad. What is it?"

"Do this more often. Whenever you feel like it, don't hesitate to come in here . . . for a chat like this, or just to get something off your chest. It never hurts to talk things over." He smiled, warmly.

"Thanks for the invitation, Dad. I won't hesitate. And that's a promise."

As Pete walked down the hall to his room he felt a lot better. He was not happy that his father was in this kind of situation, but he was pleased that the two of them could talk like this. He hadn't really done much or said much to cheer his father up. He had just listened, but his father had seemed to brighten from the moment he entered his room. He had really been glad to see him. Pete shook his head in wonder. He had always wanted to be his father's friend—and now maybe he was.

Supper was over. Pete's father had left with his reassembled vacuum cleaner, and Pete was resting on the patio. Patty had not eaten supper with them. As was getting to be usual, she had eaten supper with the Goobermans. He heard the phone ring.

"If that's Frenchy," he called in to his mother, "tell him I'm ready and to come on over."

Pete's mother appeared in the doorway of the patio. "It's not Frenchy. It's Sandra."

Pete went inside and picked up the phone.

"You never called back," Sandra said.

"When?"

"You know when. The other day when you called me and I was busy."

"I didn't call back because I know a brush-off when I get it."

She paused a moment. Then she said, softly, "I'm sorry, Pete. I was just being mean."

"Well . . . that's your privilege, I guess."

"I'm sorry, Pete."

"Let's forget it, Sandra."

"I'm going bowling later. Why don't you drop down and help me keep score?"

"Keep score?"

"You used to like that. Remember?"

"That was before you got hypersensitive about Patty."

"That was before Patty and Gooberman started going steady again, too."

He grinned. "Do you still like her, Pete."

"Sure. We're just like a normal brother and sister. We fight all the time."

"I'm going bowling around nine. Maybe I'll see you there."

"Maybe."

As he hung up, the doorbell rang. He turned and saw Frenchy through the door. Swiftly, Pete went over his options for the evening. Before supper Frenchy had called, and they had made plans to go to the stock-car races in Dunhill. He could go as planned or stay home and help Sandra keep score.

He opened the door.

"Ready, sport?" Frenchy asked. "I can hear those stocks revving up from here."

"Sure. Wait'll I get my jacket. Can I drive? I hate the way you drive with that cast."

"Old Leadfoot," Frenchy admitted with a sigh. "Okay. You can drive. I get myself nervous, too."

Pete stepped to the hall closet for his jacket.

Chapter Seven

ON THE WAY back from the Speedway, however, it was Frenchy who drove. Inspired by the skillful driving he had witnessed, he had insisted on taking the wheel. Pete had both feet firmly planted on the floor of the car, both hands braced solidly, and his seat belt as snug as he could get it.

"Slow down to the speed of light, will you?" Pete asked finally.

They were approaching a curve, and Frenchy's cast was still resting heavily on the accelerator. Frenchy was steering with one hand on the wheel, His other resting on the roof. There was a wild grin on his face.

"Nervous?" he asked.

"Of course I am."

Frenchy took his hands off the wheel. "Look, Ma! No hands!"

"You mean no brains, you nut! We're approaching a curve!"

"Maybe if we both lean, I won't have to steer."

But even as he spoke, Frenchy placed both hands firmly on the wheel and pulled his cast off the accelerator, allowing the car to slow as it entered the curve. But as soon as they were into it, he kicked his cast back onto the accelerator. The car picked up speed quickly, its tail straightened, and it shot out of the curve as heavy and flat as an iron.

"Frenchy," Pete said, "you are a funny guy. I like your sense of humor and all the rest of it. But behind the wheel is no place to clown. If you keep this up, I'm going to get out and walk."

"Chicken?"

"That's right."

"Okay. Okay."

Frenchy pushed his cast off the accelerator. As the car slowed again to a more reasonable speed, Pete leaned back and relaxed for the first time since Frenchy had climbed into the car.

"Where to?" asked Frenchy as they entered the Canton town limits not long after.

"The bowling alley," Pete answered immediately.

"Never fear. Frenchy will get you there."

And he did.

But Pete was in a hurry all of a sudden and waited with some impaticnce as Frenchy parked the car in the lot and clambered out of the car. Once inside the alleys, he went directly to the head of them and looked down the length of the place. On the next to last alley, Pete saw Sandra lining up a shot.

When he got to the head of her alley, he found her scoreboard, sat down behind it, and took up a felt pen. She was working on a spare, and from the looks of her score sheets, she had been bowling for a very long time.

She got a split on her spare and ended with an eight. He was putting it down when she turned.

"Oh, hi, Pete!"

He smiled at her. "Hello, yourself."

"Took you some time to get here."

"Well, I got here."

"Want a game?"

"Sure."

Frenchy had not sat down. "I guess I'll drive on home," he said, winking broadly at Pete.

"Take it easy, you screwball," said Pete.

"Sure. Don't worry about me."

As Frenchy left, Sandra sat down beside Pete. "How have things been, Pete?"

She was wearing a blue jumper with a blue jersey blouse. She looked nice and cool, though she must have been bowling for at least a couple of hours.

"Let's not bowl," he said. "Let's go over to a table and get a Coke."

"Sure. Just let me finish this string."

Pete kept score—and it was a good one. One-ninety-six. He ripped off the sheets and headed for the desk as Sandra gathered up her coat.

They found a table in a quiet corner, as far as Pete could get from the jukebox. "Well," he said, "it's good to see you again, Sandra. Thanks for calling me."

"And thanks for finally getting here."

"Sometimes," he said thoughtfully, "it isn't always so easy to do the right thing."

She smiled—ruefully, he thought. "I know, Pete. How're things going?"

"Lousy."

"Lousy?"

He nodded gloomily. "All down the line."

"Oh, things can't be that bad, Pete."

"I walked out on football practice this afternoon. I've had it, Sandra. Up to here. And then there's my father. He's not doing so hot as a vacuum cleaner salesman. I might have to go to work or even the Navy if he doesn't begin to bring in some money—at least more than he's bringing in right now."

"The Navy? Oh, Pete, you're not serious!"

"Why not? A good technical college is out of the question now. Besides, I could learn a good technical trade in the Navy."

"But would they let you in without a high school diploma?"

"I can graduate this January if I want. I've got enough credits to get my diploma. I just won't take German or Advanced Calculus. The Navy doesn't want dropouts, Sandra. You're right about that. And they've got a real fine bunch of technical programs. When I'm eighteen I might go into nuclear propulsion." Pete decided he wouldn't tell her about the necessity for a six-year hitch.

"Pete, this is all so wild. I never heard you mention the Navy before. Are you sure this is what you want?"

"All I know now, Sandra, is that I'm fed up with the team, fed up with school—and I'm worried about Dad. It's hard to know what to do. But the Navy looks like a golden opportunity."

"Are you sure you're not just giving up, Pete?"

"Look, sometimes 'giving up,' as you call it, is just being realistic. What's worse than fouling up all the time, for Pete's sake—just because you don't have the good sense to give up and let someone else take over." He leaned forward, aware suddenly that he had at last found words to express the frustration that had been building up within him for the past weeks.

"Let's take college. All of a sudden college graduates are having a tough time finding jobs when they graduate. Right?"

"I suppose so, Pete. But times will get better."

"Sure. Maybe they will. But how am I going to get money to go to college?"

"You could get a scholarship."

"Look. As soon as Frenchy gets his cast taken off this week, I'll be out of a job. I can go back on the line. But the guy who's taken my place is doing great. Then what kind of a season record will I have compiled, anyway? Most of the time I've just fouled-up as a middle linebacker who couldn't make an open-field tackle. And *that's* going to be my record. I might be lucky and have a few good games when I get back on the line, but that's not going to make any difference really. Any scouts from the colleges are going to look right past me. Guys like Kowalski get the headlines—and Gooberman. Foul-ups like myself—all we can hope for is a pat on the back and our letter."

"That used to be enough for some."

"Sure. And it's enough for me. But don't you see—I'm not going to be able to go to college on *that.* So it's the Navy or a job—if I get a high enough number in the draft. Either way, I quit playing games and go to work."

"You make it sound so—hopeless."

"No, realistic. Besides, weren't you the one who

was always telling me what a nutty thing it was to go chasing a football up and down a field every Saturday afternoon?"

"Well, maybe I've changed some of my ideas, Pete. I've been doing a lot of thinking myself these past weeks."

He looked at her. "They've been lonely for me too, Sandra."

"Have they, Pete?"

Pete nodded, surprised himself at this sudden admission.

"Pete, you're just down now because you're having a few reversals. That's all. Once you block a few kicks and make a couple of open-field tackles, you won't feel so bad—and you won't need Sandra anymore, either."

"That's not fair, Sandra."

"Maybe it's not fair, but I think it's the truth."

Pete did not know how to reply. Everything was getting so gloomy—and complicated. Wasn't anything simple any more?"

"Let's go somewhere," he said, finishing his Coke. Sandra got up. He picked her car coat off the back of her chair and helped her put it on.

They were almost to the door when Patty and Gooberman came rushing in. At sight of Pete, Patty came to a sudden halt, her eyes suddenly wide with relief.

"Pete!" she cried. "You're all right!"

"Of course I'm all right," agreed Pete. "What's the matter?"

"We've just seen Frenchy's car—on Market Street," said Gooberman. "That's what's the matter!"

"Frenchy's car! Hey, you mean he's been in an accident?"

"Yes," said Gooberman grimly. "He sure has."

"Earlier your mother said you'd gone to the stock-car races with him, so we thought . . ."

"Well, where *is* Frenchy? How *is* he?"

"We don't know," said Gooberman. "All we know is someone told us they had to saw through Frenchy's cast to get him out of the wreckage."

Pete felt Sandra's fingers digging into his forearm. *Saw through Frenchy's cast!* "He must be in the hospital," cried Pete. "Let's go."

The intern looked quite solemn as he approached them from the elevator. "You want to see Frenchy Wells?"

Pete nodded. "That's right. How is he?"

"His parents are upstairs now. He'll be coming out of emergency surgery soon."

"Can we go up?" Gooberman asked.

"You'd better wait down here."

"He'll . . ." Patty swallowed. "He'll be all right, won't he?"

The intern's eyebrows went up. "That depends on what you mean by all right." He turned and started back into the elevator. "He must have been going pretty fast when he hit that lamppost."

The elevator door slid shut, and the four looked grimly, wordlessly at each other for a moment before they turned and headed for the lobby to wait.

When, more than an hour later, they saw Frenchy's parents leave the elevator, they got up and started to approach them for some word about Frenchy's condition. But the distraught look on the couple's faces caused the four of them to hold back. Without a word, they let Frenchy's parents cross the lobby and leave the hospital.

"Come on," said Pete, as he led the way to the elevator.

As they left the elevator on the second floor and approached the desk, a nurse looked up. She frowned as she caught sight of them and was about to stop them when the intern who had spoken to them downstairs appeared from one of the wards.

"That's all right, nurse," he said.

Then the man beckoned to them.

"You can stay only a few minutes, I'm afraid," he

told them as he led them into Frenchy's room. "He's been given a sedative. You won't have long."

Pete nodded.

"Thanks," said Patty.

And then Pete saw Frenchy. He seemed to be covered entirely with casts or bandages. Even his face and head were swathed in bandages.

The four of them were so stunned by what they saw that they could not utter a sound. They just stood there staring.

"Hi!" came feebly from a hole under Frenchy's nose. "Don't stand there and gape! Say something. It's not as bad as it looks. Just cuts and abrasions, sprains, and a dislocated shoulder!"

"Oh, my gosh," said Patty. "Can you move, Frenchy?"

"Sure. But please don't make me laugh."

In spite of himself Pete found he was smiling. Then he caught the smile and said, "What about your leg? Someone said they had to cut through the cast to get you out of the wreck."

"They did. But let's not talk about that."

"Well, what happened anyway?"

"I had to drive off the road to avoid a collision and met a lamppost coming the other way."

"How fast were you going?" asked Sandra.

Frenchy groaned. "I wasn't driving. My cast was."

"You nut!" said Pete.

"This time it wasn't *entirely* my fault. Honest. The heel of the cast got wedged in between the brake pedal and the accelerator."

Pete could understand what had happened all right, remembering the way Frenchy kept dragging his cast back and forth across the accelerator. "Maybe now you'll quit driving with a cast on your leg."

"No more driving at all," Frenchy said. "I just got the word from my parents. Not until my 21st birthday or I get married and have to go to work—whichever comes first."

"They have a point," commented Gooberman.

"I would have to say," said Frenchy, "that I have learned my lesson." His eyes looked toward Pete. "Middle linebacker is all yours, Pete. With these injuries I won't be able to play football the rest of the season."

"Oh, Frenchy!" cried Patty. "I think that's terrible."

"Look, people. I'm tired. They gave me something, and it's making me real sleepy. But before you get out of here, remember this: I'm lucky. I could have lost my life tonight, but now I'll be around for a while longer—and now I'll be a lot more careful with this life I got. Tomorrow morning if a bird lands on that windowsill out there and starts to let out with a cheep, I'll be able to hear it." He closed his eyes and leaned back on the pillow. "And from now on," he said softly, sleepily, "from now on I'll be listening."

Outside the hospital the four of them talked quietly and soberly in front of their cars. They talked for some time. Then Sandra drove Pete home—with unusual care, Pete could not help noticing.

"Good-night, Pete," she said as she pulled up in front of Pete's house.

"Good-morning, rather," said Pete. Then he looked across at Sandra. "You know what," he said. "I wish I had Frenchy's courage."

"With Frenchy's courage also goes quite a dose of foolhardiness. And besides, you've got plenty of courage anyway, Pete. Believe me. You have."

Pete was too tired to argue. He closed the door and started up the walk to his house.

Chapter Eight

THE ONLY LIGHT came from a yellow moon that hung like a giant pumpkin just over the pines. But it was enough light for Pete as he went at the tackling dummy. The dummy had been left out for him, and he'd been hitting it hard and low, driving it on its skids slowly, relentlessly all the way down the field toward the temporary bleachers on the other side of the goalposts. When he reached the stands, he planned to stop; but he still had a little way to go.

After the first hour his thighs, shoulders, and the side of his head had gotten pretty sore. Now they were just numb and heavy with sweat. And all the while he worked he kept thinking what Frenchy had told him last night at the hospital as he was getting ready to go home.

Tackling is 25 percent technique, 75 percent desire.

That made sense all right, but Pete had a theory that desire could be increased if you were certain you had the right technique. And that's what he was doing on this practice field, working on his technique.

He looked up. He was beyond the goalposts now and was pretty close to the first row of the bleachers; he supposed he could give up at this point if he wanted to. But he didn't want to.

He put his head down, then fixed his eye on that portion of the dummy he had decided must be the ballcarrier's belt buckle and moved up closer, his feet apart, his back straight. Then he charged, hitting the dummy with his shoulder, waiting until the impact before grappling it to him. He continued to drive hard and still harder, feeling the skids of the dummy moving slowly over the now damp grass.

When he pulled himself upright and looked again at the bleachers, he decided three more tackles should do it.

It took not three but four tackles before the dummy's skid stopped at the base of the first row of bleacher seats. Pete stood up. He was dripping with perspiration. His whole body was trembling slightly, and even as he stood there, he could still feel the dummy's thick padding thrusting against his shoulder. When he put his hand up to the side of his face, the skin felt raw. A rivulet of sweat exploded from his eyebrow and crept, burning, into the corner of his eye. He tried to wipe it away with the back of his hand, but it was dirty and sweaty and didn't help at all. He took off his helmet, and—squinting—used his sleeve to wipe his eyes clear.

Then he turned and looked down the field—better than a hundred yards. His breath was no longer coming in sharp gasps, but his heart was still thudding in his throat. Would all this help any? Would he still get buck fever the moment he closed with a ballcarrier in the open?

"That was some workout!"

Pete whirled. In the far corner of the bleachers, way up on top, Sandra was sitting. He hadn't noticed her in the darkness. She stood up and started down the bleachers carefully.

He started toward her as she stepped out onto the field. "How long have you been there?"

"About an hour."

"Who told you I was here?"

"Gooberman. He said you had asked the coach to leave the tackling dummy out. How do you feel?"

"Exhausted."

"You should be. That's how I feel from just watching you."

"You got your car?"

She smiled. "Of course."

"I'm going in to shower. I'll be out in about fifteen minutes."

"I'll wait in the car. It's in the parking lot in back of the gym."

Peter nodded and trotted heavily toward the gymnasium.

As Sandra drove out of the parking lot, she glanced at Pete. "You certainly don't act like someone who's ready to throw in the towel."

"You mean you don't think I'm going to quit school and join the Navy?"

"It certainly doesn't look that way."

"Well, I am. I've made up my mind. I've even brought the papers home for my folks to sign."

"Pete!"

"Tomorrow night will be my last game. That's why I want to do it right."

"Pete! You're not serious."

He looked at her. "Of course I am. When I told my father that he wasn't going to have to worry about sending me to college, it was . . . well, it was like I had taken a great weight off his shoulders."

Sandra said nothing for a while. Then she said, "What's he doing? Still selling vacuum cleaners?"

"That's right. But lately he's been talking about going on welfare, and I haven't seen his kit anywhere." Pete tried to keep the bitterness out of his tone.

"Welfare?"

"That job they were holding open for him at the light company is gone. And there are no other jobs. Especially for men as old as my father. He'll do all right on welfare, though. Disability insurance will soon be coming in from the light company."

"But Pete . . . the Navy!"

He laughed. "So what's wrong with that? At least it will get me out of here. All of a sudden I want to shake off the dust of this town—but fast."

They were pulling up in front of his house. As Sandra braked the car, she looked across the seat at him. "You're running away, Pete."

"What do you mean, running away? That's not fair—not fair at all."

"Well, I'm sorry, Pete. But I think you are. You're ashamed of your father going on welfare, and you're hurting because Patty is going steady with Gooberman, and you're a flop this season on the football field. So you're going to run away and join the Navy. Well, lots of luck."

"Now, look, Sandra," protested Pete. He was stung by her words. "You don't know me well enough to say that. There's a big wide world out there, and I want to see it. I'm not running away. I'm running *to* something—a career in the United States Navy."

Sandra smiled, as if she had said all she had intended to say—or needed to say. Feeling uneasy, as if he had really lost an important argument, Pete got out of the car and slammed the door.

Sandra put the car in gear. The rear ties squealed as she gunned the motor. He watched her go, then shrugged and went inside.

His father was sitting in front of the television set. He didn't look up as Pete entered. Pete looked at the gray, flickering screen. It was a rerun his father was watching—a loud family comedy. His father never used to watch these kinds of programs, but this was the second day in a row Pete had come home to find his father settled in front of the television set.

"Hi, Dad."

"Hi, Pete."

"Where's Mom?"

"In the kitchen with Patty."

Pete went into the kitchen and walked straight to the refrigerator. Patty and his mother were sitting at the table, talking quietly. As he took the carton of milk out, he glanced at them.

"Talking about that great guy, Gooberman?"

"No, we weren't talking, Pete," Patty replied, her voice hushed and serious.

Pete poured the milk into a tall glass, gulping down the whole glass without a pause. He placed the empty glass in the sink. "What *are* you two conspirators discussing then?"

"Your father," his mother said.

"What about him? He seems happy enough, now that he's discovered television."

"Please, Pete," his mother said sharply. "That's not kind, not kind at all."

Patty spoke up then. "Sandra's father called."

"Oh? What did he want?"

"He offered Dad a job," his mother told him. "He said he couldn't hold it open for him much longer."

"What'd Dad say?"

"He turned it down."

For a moment Pete had felt hope; now he felt only resignation. "I'm going upstairs," he said. "I'm bushed."

"Pete . . . ?"

"What, Mother?"

"Would you . . . would you go in and speak to Dad?"

"Why should I? It's his decision to make."

"Is it?"

"Sure, Mom. Of course it is."

"Do you *want* him to make this kind of a decision?"

"It doesn't matter what I want, Mom. I can't make Dad do something he doesn't want to do, can I?"

Patty shook her head. "I can't understand him. What's *wrong* with him?"

"Have you watched him walk lately?"

Just then the front doorbell rang. "I'll get it," Pete said wearily, glad for the interruption.

It was Frenchy at the door. He was leaning on a new set of crutches. A bandage was stuck across his forehead at a rakish angle. And his right foot and leg were in a brand new cast. Aside from that, there was no sign of his other injuries—until he swung in past Pete. Then it was that Pete noticed how he winced. His bruised left leg was bothering him, too.

"First day out," Frenchy said. "So guess who I look up. You should feel honored."

"Come in," said Pete, closing the door behind him. "Go right on into the kitchen. Just don't trip over anything."

As Pete followed behind Frenchy, he could not help wondering if he would ever see his friend without crutches, and indeed if perhaps Frenchy himself would not be lost without them. He got around with such marvelous dexterity on them that they had almost become a part of his personality. Still, it was only a momentary thought, and one that Pete didn't particularly like. It would be a good day indeed when he saw Frenchy striding along without crutches.

"Aha!" cried Frenchy, as he swung into the kitchen and saw Patty. "A worthy opponent! How about a game of ping pong, Patty?"

"You must be kidding!" she cried with a laugh.

"You're right," said Frenchy, sobering at once and turning to Pete. "It wouldn't be fair. I'd beat her terribly. She'd be lucky to make a point."

Patty laughed again. "Now you're not going to goad me into playing with you."

"Why not?"

"Well . . ." She looked at his crutches.

At that moment Pete caught—from deep within Frenchy's eyes—a look of such despondency that he looked quickly away. And in that same instant, he realized, he had glimpsed the anguish over his accident that Frenchy's happy-go-lucky manner now worked so hard to keep hidden.

"Forget the crutches!" Frenchy cried gaily. "I've been sitting in a hospital bed. I need some exercise."

"You don't want to overdo it," said Pete's mother.

"Let him," Pete heard himself say suddenly. "Frenchy needs exercise, not sympathy."

"Right!" said Frenchy, and he swung out of the kitchen onto the patio.

With a shrug, Patty followed.

The third game was almost over. Pete had sat in a lawn chair and watched each stroke. Patty won the first and second games easily, but that wasn't the point. Pete had been deeply impressed at the tenacious way in which Frenchy had hung in. It was obvious that Frenchy—though he might be his worse enemy at times—had a tenacity, a courage that made him thoroughly admirable. He didn't seem to know what it meant to quit.

Pete had spent a couple of afternoons in Frenchy's room this past week and had finally gotten to know the real Frenchy Wells, the one that lived behind the wise cracks and the jolly smile. What he'd found out had really sobered him. It seemed that Frenchy was not really the laughing, carefree boy that everyone thought he was. He was in reality a deep and quite serious young man. To Pete's surprise, Frenchy admitted that until he was eight years old he had spent his youth moving from one foster home to another—until he was finally adopted by his present foster parents.

"I never really knew who I was," he told Pete. "And I figured maybe I'd done something wrong back there somewhere, and that was why nobody wanted me. That was the only way I could explain what was happening to me. So when people came to look at me—you know, like I was something they might like to buy—I decided I'd become a real funny guy, smiling all the time, making jokes and clowning around. And it worked, Pete. I finally got adopted. And you know my folks. They're great . . . but still I keep wondering . . . what really happened back there? What had I done wrong?"

When Pete tried to convince Frenchy that he couldn't have done anything wrong, Frenchy had agreed readily enough.

"Oh, sure, Pete," he said, grinning suddenly. "It was just bad luck. I know that. No one's fault really.

But still, Pete, I just can't get rid of that feeling . . ."

And now, as Pete watched Frenchy swatting hilariously with ping pong paddle at the elusive ball, he could not help but wonder if even during this wild moment Frenchy wasn't still wondering what he had done wrong.

And yet he didn't let on. He kept going. And kept laughing.

"Hey!" Patty cried, as she tried desperately to reach one of Frenchy's serves.

"See that?" Frenchy demanded of Pete. "That gives me eleven points. Now I make my move!"

Pete laughed and got up suddenly. "I'm going inside. Play on, you nut. Play on."

Pete's mother was busy with supper. He went past her without a word and on into the living room. His father was still watching television. Pete walked over to the set and turned it off.

His father looked at him sharply. "What did you do that for? Turn that back on!"

"I want to talk to you, Dad. It's important."

"Well, don't come in like that, turning off the set. That being a little rude, don't you think?"

"Yes, I'm sorry, Dad, I didn't mean to be rude. It's just that not so long ago, you told me I should come see you anytime and not hesitate to speak right up and tell you what I think. You made me promise I would. Remember?"

His father smiled slightly. "Okay. I remember. What is it then?"

"I understand Sandra's father called about a job today."

"That's right."

"I want to know why you didn't take it."

"It's inside work."

Pete looked around the room and then at the television set. "So is this."

"I'll find something outside. You watch. Soon as my back gets better."

"I think you should take the job, Dad."

His father looked at him. "You do, do you?"

"Just because it's Sandra's father that offered the job, I don't think you should turn it down."

"I don't want any favors from your friends, Pete. I've had enough help from friends, well-meaning friends. And besides, I don't particularly like Sandra's father. He's got too much money, too much power around here to suit me."

"I thought that was the reason."

"You don't get along with Sandra yourself, Pete. You don't deny that, do you?"

"Well, it's my fault. Not hers. She's okay. A real okay person, and I've been crazy not to realize it sooner."

Pete's father snorted. "Well now. What caused this sudden change of heart?"

"I don't know for sure. Watching Frenchy out there playing ping pong on crutches may be part of it. But I know now why I acted the way I did with Sandra. I'm a snob, Dad. She's rich, so I look down on her. Like it was her fault or something that she has her own car and nice clothes. But since when is that a crime, Dad?"

The man shrugged.

"You see what I mean, Dad? I'll bet that the only reason you won't take that job is because you're a snob, too."

"You think so, do you?"

"It's a possibility, isn't it?"

"Turn the television back on and go on out to the patio. You've had your say."

Pete looked at his father for a moment. He wanted to continue the discussion, but he shrugged, turned the set back on, and started back to the patio.

He had taken his courage in his hands and had spoken to his father as honestly as he could. He had tried to make him see it the way he saw it. But perhaps he was wrong, and his father was right.

Pete stirred fitfully, then woke up. He was groggy from sleep, but awake enough to see his father standing in the open doorway.

"Hi, Dad," he managed.

His father closed the door and walked over to his bed. "Hi, Pete. Sorry to wake you. But . . . well, I've been doing some thinking—about what you said."

The man sat down on the edge of Pete's bed and looked at him for a long time. Then he cleared his throat. "Sometimes, Pete, things knock us for a loop —and we try to tell ourselves we aren't hurt. But we are. And so we don't act so hot. Like we're off course and don't know where we're going. Know what I mean?"

"I guess so, Dad."

"Anyway, it helps when we've got someone who cares which way we go. I have you and Mom. So I guess I'm pretty lucky." He left Pete then, closed the door softly, and was gone.

Pete thought a minute, smiled, and went back to sleep.

Chapter Nine

THE SAXTON CENTRAL High Comets, resplendent in their maroon and white uniforms, charged out through the aisle of pennant-waving, high-stepping cheerleaders. Once the arc lights caught their helmets, the Saxton home crowd let out a roar that caused the night air to tremble.

To the fans of Saxton Central and those of Canton as well, this game had suddenly become the season's big game, despite the fact that each team had several more games to play. Saxton Central had caught fire after their second game and had from that point on completely demoralized every opponent they faced by ridiculously lopsided scores. They were suddenly the class of the conference—unless Canton could stop them.

And that meant stopping number ten—Lars Hanson.

Pete was thinking of Hanson as he stood on the sidelines under his blue cape. Number ten was a great big Viking with enormous shoulders and outsized thighs and an unruly shock of blond hair that was only barely contained by his helmet. He looked pleasant enough except for the protruding, rocklike chin and the cold gleam in his icy blue eyes when he ran over you.

That was what Pete remembered from the year before—the one time the Saxton coach had put him in. At the time, Hanson was just a big sophomore who had just enrolled in their school, and they weren't quite sure which position to play him. They were sure now, however. Fullback.

And Pete was to key on him.

The Comets had won the toss and were about to receive the kick. Pete glanced down the line of players and saw Coach Quenton give them the nod. He sprinted out onto the field. As he went, he heard Frenchy cry out to him.

"Go get him, Pete!"

The kick was a good high one, end over end, and there was little runback by the Comet back who caught it. Pete was in on the tackle, which put the football on the Comet's fifteen.

"Okay, Pete," said Gooberman, as the Comet huddle broke. "Stay on ten. He's your man, remember. When he scratches his ear, I want you on hand to see what he's up to. Got it?"

"Sure," said Pete with a grim smile. "And thanks a lot."

The Saxton High quarterback wasn't fancy at all. On the very first play he played his ace and pitched the football out to number ten, who scooted for the right side of the line.

That was the thing about Hanson, according to all the scouting reports; he was tough, but he was also very fast. He could go inside, and he could go outside.

Pete hurdled a Comet blocker, fought off another lineman coming through to nail him, and then found nothing but daylight between him and Hanson. The big fellow veered quickly toward Pete in an obvious attempt to intimidate him.

Pete took sight on the fellow's midsection and launched himself. The impact shook Pete, but he grappled both hands around Hanson's waist and kept his legs driving hard. But he felt himself being pulled around, and then Hanson was slipping free. Pete felt a powerful fist slamming down on his shoulder; he tried to hang on, but couldn't. By that time, however, Gooberman and the rest of the team had arrived. Like a band of howling apes they gang-tackled Hanson, and the big man disappeared under a crowd of blue-and-white jerseys.

Nevertheless, he got eight yards.

"Come on. We've got to stop this guy," said Gooberman to the defensive huddle.

"What else is new," remarked Paul Christman.

The Comet huddle broke. Pete watched Hanson set himself and took a deep breath. This was going to be some game. On the snap, number ten went for a hole in the right side of the line; but the quarterback was going back into the pocket, hand held high, the football ready to fly. At the same moment Pete saw out of the corner of his eye the Comet right end breaking into the flat. He was wide open. At once Pete decided to forget Hanson.

As the end turned for the pass, Pete crossed over quickly to nail him, certain that he had diagnosed the play perfectly. But there was no pass for the end to catch. Then Pete heard the crowd break into a roar, looked back over his shoulder and saw Hanson—all alone in the secondary—gathering in the pass.

As Hanson started downfield, he simply ran over one would-be tackler and straight-armed another; then he cut swiftly to the sideline and was off. Pete turned and started belatedly after him, but it was Gooberman and Paul Christman who finally rode the big fullback out of bounds—after a gain of thirty yards.

"You were supposed to key on Hanson," Gooberman said, still breathing heavily as he joined the defensive huddle.

Pete noticed a slight cut under Gooberman's right cheekbone. "What happened?"

"I blew it."

The Comet quarterback gave his famous fullback a rest after those two openers and completed two quick passes. Then he handed off to his halfback, who got caught behind the line of scrimmage by Gooberman.

"Stay alive, Pete," said Gooberman when he got back to the huddle. "The quarterback's going to have to go to Hanson on this next play. Maybe another sweep."

Pete moved over to his middle linebacker slot to await developments. This Hanson was some football player. Even though you knew he was coming, there was little you could do to stop him. Unless . . .

Pete decided he would blitz. But he would not be aiming for the quarterback. He would go for number ten, get him *before* he could get under way.

Anticipating the snap perfectly, Pete bulled past the center and reached out for Hanson just as he was tucking away the hand-off. Hanson glanced at Pete with a look of mild surprise; then with a big swipe of his arm, he flung Pete to one side, reversed his field and headed for a hole in the line—a big one that was opening up right on schedule.

Desperately Pete reached back with one hand and grabbed Hanson's ankle. He yanked. Unfortunately, the foot came up with more force than Pete had bargained for and slammed against the side of his cheek. A shower of lights exploded deep inside his head, but he hung on tenaciously for as long as he could. It was long enough. Gooberman and two others smothered Hanson before he could pull free and exploit the big hole in the line. The trouble was, just by falling forward, he gained two yards.

"Hey," said Gooberman, looking closely at Pete's cheek. "You've really got a bruise there."

Pete could feel the numbness and ache spreading up to his eye. It was as if something heavy were growing inside his cheek.

"Anyway, you slowed him. Nice play."

Pete felt a tap on his shoulder. He turned and saw Wiley Cole, a big sophomore who was developing fast. "Coach says take a rest."

Pete ducked out of the defensive huddle and raced to the sidelines. The doctor examined Pete's cheekbone, whistled softly, and went for an ice pack. When he came back with it, he told Pete to hold it against his cheekbone.

Pete found a seat next to Frenchy and was just in time to see Hanson break through the line, turn, and catch a short pass. There were only twenty yards separating the big fullback from pay dirt by this time, and it seemed that the moment Hanson caught sight of the goal line, he became jet-propelled. Two Canton players came up to stop him, but he just ran over them. When Gooberman finally got to him on the goal line, it was too late. Hanson just carried Gooberman—as big as he was—over the goal stripe with him.

Then he slammed the ball to the ground and still standing, dumped Gooberman and trotted back to his teammates for the kick after.

"Oh, boy," said Frenchy softly. "Oh, boy."

Pete didn't say anything. He just pressed the ice pack closer to his aching cheek.

Gary West started from his twenty. In keeping with Coach Quenton's game plan, he stayed with conservative plays up the middle for short but solid gains. Kowalski carried quite often, but whenever the middle closed up, Linn Harlow got the call and went outside. Inside, then outside. On occasion, just to sweeten the pot, Gary sent short passes over the middle.

It was ball-control football, and it was working to perfection. Time was eaten up as the ball moved steadily, relentlessly upfield until it was first and ten on the eleven-yard line. Kowalski bulled his way to the two-yard line. The next play gained nothing.

Then Linn Harlow drifted almost casually into the corner of the end zone, turned and caught a soft lob from West for the tying touchdown.

Two minutes later Lars Hanson gathered in Gary West's kickoff on his fifteen, flicked one lunging tackler off him, darted through a crowd of blue-and-white jerseys, found daylight, cut to the sidelines, and rapidly outdistanced every pursuer on the field. He wasn't even puffing as he pulled up in the end zone and slammed the football to the ground.

Again Gary West started his team upfield. And again he was able to move the ball, not swiftly or spectacularly, but consistently. But then on the twelve-yard line Kowalski fumbled, and the Comets recovered.

Coach Summers appeared before Pete. "How's the cheekbone feel?"

"Okay."

Summers turned and looked nervously out onto the field. Then he looked back at Pete, pursing his lips thoughtfully. "Why don't we let Wiley stay in for you."

"Suits me."

As the coach moved off, Frenchy looked at Pete. "What's the matter with you anyway?"

"What do you mean?"

"You should have put up a squawk. You don't want Wiley to push you out of the lineup."

"At least Wiley can't do any worse than I did."

"Boy, you sound like a real winner. Come on, Pete. Be sensible. You did pretty well. All you can do with a monster like Hanson is slow him down some and pray for help. You were doing that just fine."

Pete didn't reply, but Frenchy's words made him feel somewhat better, and he leaned forward with new interest to watch his replacement as he attempted to stop Hanson. Cole was big enough, but he always seemed to be reaching for number ten just after he went by. At the conclusion of a particularly long gainer by Hanson, Coach Summers appeared again beside Pete.

"I think you'd better go in, Pete."

Pete handed the coach the ice pack and grabbed his helmet.

Gooberman's eyes seemed to light up a little when he saw Pete ducking into the huddle. As Cole bolted for the sideline, Gooberman said, "Welcome back, Pete. We need your help before Hanson turns this into a comedy."

The Comet huddle broke. The quarterback hustled up to the line. It was a second and two, and everyone in the stadium knew who was going to get the ball.

Hanson took the hand-off and plowed straight ahead. By the time Pete crashed into him, Hanson had already got his two yards. But then the fullback spun around, brought his forearm down on the top of Pete's helmet, pulled away, and was not brought down until he had gained another four yards.

Pete's head was still buzzing when he reached the defensive huddle.

"My gosh," he said to Gooberman. "That guy couldn't have just enrolled in Saxton High. The coach must have gone out and trapped him."

"Maybe," replied Gooberman grimly. "But we've still got to hang in there and stop him."

On the next play, the Comet quarterback faked a hand-off to Hanson, then whirled and raced back into his pocket. Pete had stayed with Hanson and was closing on him until he saw the quarterback getting set to pass to one of his backs on the other side of the field. Then he pulled up—not wishing to tangle with Hanson unless he absolutely had to.

At once Hanson shifted into high and broke past Pete into the clear. Pete had been finessed. The quarterback squared around to pass to Hanson. Extending himself to his limit, Pete raced after Hanson and flung himself through the air, as if he were sliding home from third base. His feet just did manage to tangle with Hanson's, and the big fullback tripped and went tumbling out of bounds.

Pete, flat on his back, glanced over his shoulder and saw the quarterback swing around again and make a desperate heave into the flat, aiming for his flanker. But it was a hurried, wobbly pass; and out of nowhere Gooberman appeared, leaped into the air, and caught the ball. Once he had possession, he reversed his field, smashed past one would-be tackler, then lit out downfield.

There was only the quarterback to stop him and Gooberman made mincemeat out of him. After that it was a footrace. But Gooberman knew what this touchdown could mean and maintained what for him was a sizzling pace. Only when he crossed the goal line did he stagger a couple of times and then collapse.

Pete was cheering with the rest of his teammates when he found himself staring at a referee. On the ground beside the referee there was a handkerchief—a red one. The referee pointed to Pete.

"Tripping," he said. Then he blew his whistle and indicated the flag.

Pete's heart sank. Tripping! The play would be called back. Gooberman's brilliant interception and run for a touchdown had gone for nothing!

The Comets accepted the penalty with great relief; there were, in fact, grins on their faces as they returned to their huddle and watched the referee step off the distance.

Gooberman wheezed up to Pete, his face a picture of frustration. Then he shook his head. He seemed ready to hurl his helmet to the ground. Pete just looked away. He understood how the big linebacker felt. He felt the same way.

Before the Comets could get off the next play, the gun sounded, ending the half.

On the way off the field, Gooberman overtook him. "As a middle linebacker, Pete, you really are something. Tripping! Maybe the Navy is the best place for you at that."

All Pete could do was nod. He didn't really see how he could argue with that judgment.

Chapter Ten

SLUMPED IN FRONT of his locker, Pete looked up in time to see Frenchy swing into the locker room. Frenchy took a long look at Pete, then, shaking his head sorrowfully, swung over beside him.

"Don't feel so bad," he told Pete. "It could be a lot worse." He eased down beside Pete and leaned his crutches back against the locker next to him. "Just remember one thing. You tripped up Hanson, all right. But if you hadn't, he'd have caught that pass in full stride and been down that field and in to score for sure."

"You're right," Pete admitted. "But don't forget. I let Hanson get past me in the first place."

"Okay. Okay. Forget the postmortems. Did you know that your father is in the stands?"

"Where's he sitting?"

"Back of the bench. And guess who he's with."

"Who?"

"Sandra and her father. He's sitting right between them. I would say that the three of them are quite emotionally involved in the outcome of this game."

Pete's father and Sandra's father . . . sitting together in the stands? Could that mean . . .

Gooberman approached, looking rather grim.

"Hi, Goober," said Pete. "Still mad?"

"Sorry about that crack, Pete. Anyway I just finished talking with Coach Summers. He thinks it would be a good idea to put Wiley back in as middle linebacker. I'll be the one who keys on Hanson."

"How come?" said Pete.

"Your cheekbone. It's swelled up pretty badly. Probably affecting your vision."

"*That's* not the reason, Goober."

Gooberman shrugged and walked off.

Pete watched him go, aware suddenly that his cheekbone *was* throbbing.

Just then both coaches entered the locker room, ready to blast. Pete sighed and leaned forward to listen.

As Pete, sitting next to Frenchy, watched Gooberman keying on Hanson and Wiley Cole filling his spot at middle linebacker, he couldn't help noticing the improvement. Gooberman was really holding Hanson. The result was that for the first time the Comet quarterback was forced to punt.

Gary West took over on his forty and again drove downfield with short gainers that finally pushed the ball over the goal line with less than a minute left in the third period. The kick was good, and the final period began with both teams tied at fourteen all.

As the final period progressed, however, it became apparent to Pete that even the mighty Gooberman was beginning to have his problems containing Hanson. Finally on an end run with Hanson carrying the ball, Gooberman collided with Hanson with such force that even the Saxton fans groaned in sympathy as Gooberman went down. It was almost as if Gooberman had stumbled in front of a bulldozer. Nevertheless, the formidable Hanson *was* stopped without a gain.

Gooberman, however, got up rather slowly; and as he headed for the defensive huddle, Pete was sure he saw a slight limp.

On the next play Gooberman started out quickly to cover Hanson, as the fullback was sent out as a decoy, but it was immediately apparent that Gooberman could not keep up with Hanson. Luckily the quarterback threw a short pass to his flanker back, who then dropped the ball for an incomplete pass.

Pete stood up as Gooberman turned and began to limp off the field.

Summers came charging down the bench toward Pete. "Get in there, Pete. Take middle linebacker. Put Cole in as monsterman and *you* key on Hanson."

Pete raced out onto the field and barely had time to give the instructions to Cole before the Comet huddle broke. He had learned something watching Gooberman. Gooberman had covered Hanson close enough, but not too close. And not until it was certain Hanson was to get a pass or had received a hand-off or pitchout did he get any closer. Pete decided he had perhaps tried to keep too close before.

On the snap the quarterback handed off to his flanker coming around. Hanson, Pete noted, was heading in the other direction, moving casually, effortlessly—but fast. Pete—on the other side of the line—kept up with Hanson, drifting over to meet him if he should suddenly decide to take off down the sideline stripe.

Then Hanson did just that. But he could not shake Pete, who found he was able to match him stride for stride. And then Pete saw the football in the air. The flanker back had thrown it to Hanson on the option. It was too far over for Pete to knock down, but it had not been thrown well and did not lead Hanson sufficiently. Pete timed his tackle perfectly, and just as Hanson touched the football, he hit him belt high with all the concentrated fury he had been teaching himself recently.

Hanson gasped and collapsed sideways, the football flying loose and out of bounds. Pete kept driving, nevertheless, until Hanson was down, flat on his back with Pete on top.

It was the best tackle Pete had made all season, and the authority of it stunned the crowd.

On the next play the flanker back got the ball again, but this time he kept it and made about four yards.

Third and six.

"Pass!" whispered Pete to Cole. "Expect a pass. Blitz!"

Cole nodded.

On the snap the quarterback went back into his pocket; the ball held high. Hanson drifted out to the right. Back and still farther back went the quarterback with Cole trying desperately to get him after missing him on his first overeager rush. And then Pete saw that the blockers were forming in front of Hanson.

"Screen!" he yelled. "Screen!"

But even as he yelled, the football was in the air. Swiftly Pete threaded through Hanson's covey of blockers and leaped for it. He knew that if he missed the ball, Hanson would catch it and be off downfield with more blockers ahead of him than he had ever needed in a game this year.

But the football snugged tightly between the palms of Pete's hands, and he came down with it tucked firmly under the crook of his right arm. He felt one tackler strike him a glancing blow on the side and fall off, dodged inside to elude another, and kept moving. It was amazing how fast the stripes passed under his feet—and he caught again the exhileration he used to feel when he was a fullback on offense.

And then a mountain fell on him from behind. He tucked the ball into his middle and collapsed. After the whistle, he rolled over dazedly and got slowly to his feet. Hanson had made the tackle, and Pete found himself staring into the fullback's cold blue eyes.

"Nice tackle," Pete managed.

"I owed it to you." Hanson's iron face cracked—and he almost smiled.

Pete looked for the sideline marker and found that he had made it all the way to the fifteen. Not too bad.

And then a storm of hands were pounding him on the back while an incoherent mob of teammates steered him back toward the Canton bench.

Gary West did the best he could with this opportunity, but all he could manage after three plays that got nowhere was a field goal to put Canton ahead by a score of 17 to 14, with three minutes left in the final period. The home fans were ominously silent. Only the thin band of Canton rooters could be heard as they made up in enthusiasm what they lacked in size.

Pete turned as he slipped off his cape and waved to his father in the stands.

"Don't relax now, friend," said Frenchy. "This night's entertainment isn't over yet."

A moment or two later, as Pete picked himself up off the wet grass, he realized just how true that warning of Frenchy's was. The Comet quarterback had sent a short pass to his flanker. Pete had left Hanson to chase the flanker and had been cut down neatly. The play had gained fifteen yards, which put the Comets inside Canton's fifty-yard line with a first and ten.

And there was still a little more than two minutes left.

"We've got to hold! We've got to hold!" Pete told the defensive huddle.

"We know, Pete. We know," said Gomer Peterson.

And as Pete set himself a moment later, he realized that holding meant stopping Hanson. On the snap Hanson took a hand-off and started into the center of the line. Pete met him head on, dug in grimly, and waited for help. It was not long in coming, but Hanson still made four yards.

The next play opened up with a fake up the middle to the left halfback, after which Hanson took the pitchout and went for the right side of the line. As Pete kept pace, he saw the flanker back cutting through the line to take him out. Pete tried to avoid the back, but he was not entirely successful. As he went down, Hanson cut over his falling body. But Pete kept his eye on Hanson's flying feet, and as Hanson soared over him, Pete reached out with both hands and grabbed one of the big fullback's shoes. This time, as Pete hit the ground, he hugged Hanson's shoe to his chest.

It was like hooking a moving train, but Hanson went down heavily and was a little slow in getting up. This time he made only two yards.

With four yards to go for a first down, it was obvious that the quarterback would have to give it to his star fullback. Pete looked at Cole. "Blitz the quarterback just in case."

Cole nodded.

On the snap the quarterback handed off to Hanson. It looked like a weak side power sweep. But as soon as Pete moved over to meet him, Hanson whirled and lateraled back to the quarterback. Pete pulled up and glanced downfield.

All he could see were two Comet receivers, each of them well covered.

Then he looked back at the quarterback just in time to see him send a short pass right back to Hanson, who had slipped quickly past Pete and was now well in the clear. Pete's heart flipped as Hanson reached up and pulled the ball down over his shoulder, not missing a stride.

It was football at its wildest—but it had worked. Hanson was in the clear, heading for pay dirt.

Pete started after him, straining every muscle, holding nothing back because this was the ball game. Christman came up fast and tried to nail Hanson, but number ten swerved at the last minute, and Christman caught nothing but a piece of flying heel. Then Art Randall took a shot. But Hanson cut inside, changing direction with such speed that Art found nothing but air.

But Pete was gaining. He had sensed that Hanson would have to cut inside to avoid Randall and had gained considerably on Hanson when he did cut. He was now only a full stride behind Hanson and couldn't wait much longer; his breath was coming in sharp, painful gasps.

One more stride he dared; then he reached out and pushed off. He caught Hanson about the waist, driving in viciously. But his arms slipped down past Hanson's waist, and the battering, pistonlike blows of Hanson's pumping thighs threatened to shake Pete loose; but he tightened his grip, pulled his head in under the fullback's left arm, and then drove again into the fellow's side.

He heard Hanson gasp, felt him try to beat Pete off,

and then felt him stumble. As he did so, Pete reached around for the ball. He felt it loosen a second before both of them hit the ground.

It was Gomer Peterson who fell on the loose football—and a second or two later, the game was over.

Sandra was standing in the parking lot, Pete beside her. Sandra's father and Pete's were standing by the family car, still talking excitedly. As the two of them got into the big car, Pete could hear his father's low chuckle. A moment later they drove off, Pete's father waving to them as they left.

"They sounded like old friends," said Pete to Sandra, as they started for her car.

She smiled. "They both like to watch the Giants and the Yankees. And they both work hard and love their family. Looks like they have a lot in common. Know what I mean?"

"Yes," Pete said, grinning. "I read you loud and clear. Now. Do you remember what you told me in the bowling alley—that all I needed to do was block a few kicks and make a couple of open-field tackles and I wouldn't feel things were so hopeless?"

She smiled. "Yes, I remember."

"Well, you were right. It looks like I'm going to finish the season as middle linebacker."

"I'm glad, Pete."

"But you were wrong about one thing."

"What's that?"

"You also said then I wouldn't need you. Sandra, a guy will always need his friends—and his girl."

Sandra didn't answer. She didn't need to. The look in her eyes told Pete what he wanted to know. He'd passed through a kind of trial this season—and somehow he'd gotten through it—he, his father, and Frenchy, too.

There'd be other seasons in the future, some not so tough, but some a lot tougher. But he'd drive hard, keep his shoulder low, and he'd make it. After all, he'd be the middle linebacker for the rest of the season. He was getting the hang of it now. He liked it, in fact. Maybe he *would* make a name for himself—and get some kind of scholarship.

Be patient, Pete, he told himself as he took Sandra's arm and started toward her car. *Things are looking up. Today's the first day of the rest of you life.*